Annoyance Turned To Anger

as he took a step toward her. "You realize you're throwing away what we have without a backward look."

Jade faced him squarely, almost welcoming the release of the emotion roiling within her. "I know I'm not going to try to live up to the image you have of me. You want more than I can give."

Of all the ways she could have chosen to escape him, this was the most painful. "Damn it," he swore, "I'm not trying to cage you."

"Aren't you?" Jade's brows rose in mock surprise. "It felt like that to me. You've got yourself convinced I need someone who understands me and I'll be just like any other woman."

Russ stared at her, realizing he had lost before he even had a chance to win. "You're so wrong, Jade. And so am I. I never should have taken you. You're like the wild creatures I care for. Except that your compulsion to roam is a trap of steel that will never release you. No one can own you, or even love you, for you won't allow it. Let's just finish the job you're here to do, so we can both be free...."

Dear Reader:

Welcome! You hold in your hand a Silhouette Desire—your ticket to a whole new world of reading pleasure.

A Silhouette Desire is a sensuous, contemporary romance about passions, problems and the ultimate power of love. It is about today's woman—intelligent, successful, giving—but it is also the story of a romance between two people who are strong enough to follow their own individual paths, yet strong enough to compromise, as well.

These books are written by, for and about every woman that you are—wife, mother, sister, lover, daughter, career woman. A Silhouette Desire heroine must face the same challenges, achieve the same successes, in her story as you do in your own life.

The Silhouette reader is not afraid to enjoy herself. She knows when to take things seriously and when to indulge in a fantasy world. With six books a month, Silhouette Desire strives to meet her many moods, but each book is always a compelling love story.

Make a commitment to romance—go wild with Silhouette Desire!

Best,

Isabel Swift
Senior Editor & Editorial Coordinator

SARA CHANCE
To Tame the Wind

Silhouette Desire

Published by Silhouette Books New York

America's Publisher of Contemporary Romance

SILHOUETTE BOOKS
300 East 42nd St., New York, N.Y. 10017

ISBN: 0-373-05430-0

First Silhouette Books printing June 1988

Printed in the U.S.A.

Books by Sara Chance

Silhouette Desire

Her Golden Eyes #46
Home at Last #83
This Wildfire Magic #107
A Touch of Passion #183
Look Beyond Tomorrow #244
Where the Wandering Ends #357
Double Solitaire #388
Shadow Watch #406
To Tame the Wind #430

SARA CHANCE

lives on Florida's Gold Coast. With the ocean two minutes from home, a boat in the water in the backyard and an indoor swimming pool three feet from her word processor, is it any wonder she loves swimming, fishing and boating? Asked why she writes romance fiction she replies, "I live it and believe in it. After all, I met and married my husband, David, in less than six weeks." That was two teenage daughters and twenty years ago. Two of Sara's Desires, *Her Golden Eyes* and *A Touch of Passion*, were nominated by *Romantic Times* in the Best Desires category for their publishing years.

One

I'm going to boil you in oil, Daryl Worth," Jade Hendricks muttered grimly, slapping at another giant mosquito perched on her bare thigh. "Do you a favor, my hind foot! The next time one of your fair-haired boys has to give up an assignment that you've worked and slaved to get him, you can find someone else besides me to act as substitute."

The whoosh of air of a passing semi made her grab the steering wheel of her rented compact car as it tried to buck off the narrow road. A wide drainage ditch half-full of murky water was on her left, and to her right stretched a swampy pasture that was probably responsible for breeding most of Florida's hungry insect population. Neither place appealed to her as a parking spot for the wayward car.

Her agent, Daryl, and his fiancée, Irene, had a lot to answer for, she decided, striving for rationality. If they weren't such good friends, and if she hadn't seen Daryl's need of a favor as a graceful escape from Irene's not-so-subtle matchmaking, she'd still be in New York City enjoying a well-earned break. Instead, she had foregone the rest she needed from the hectic pace of the past few months and the nonstop journey that had brought her halfway around the world. She had climbed onto a plane to work for a man who, by Daryl's account, could match her in intensity and commitment. Russell Blackwell, the client, had been very demanding about the qualifications of the person he wanted to photograph and write his story. Daryl had been determined she would do the assignment.

So now Jade, a globe-trotting photographer and writer, was on her way to a ranch located in the middle of nowhere. She had been in worse places. Usually she took the demands of her profession in stride. But not today.

Blowing at the tendrils of hair sticking to her forehead, Jade mentally cursed the humidity that wrapped around her like a soggy, woolen blanket on a hot, midsummer day. She was accustomed to heat, having spent a good deal of her career in deserts and jungles. But she had never grown used to the draining effects of humidity. Beyond pinning her hair up and wearing lightweight cottons there was little she could do to improve her lot.

"That car agency might be at the top of the list in popularity, but in my book it belongs at minus five million," she grumbled, squinting against the glare of the sun off the white car hood.

She poked her sunglasses more securely on her glistening nose and tried to think of something pleasant.

An oasis, palm trees and a light evening breeze on a desert-scented night floated through her mind. For one blessed second the image hovered around her, bringing a welcome relief from the steamy reality. Then another truck swished by, nearly catapulting her into a lazy herd of cows grazing on the randomly spotted areas poking above the flooded ground.

"Damn," she swore in exasperation. "The radio's on the fritz and the air conditioner's out. I'm on a godforsaken asphalt cow path headed for nowhere in a land where the bugs are bigger than the birds. Traveling first class my horse's rear end. I'm going to take Daryl's briefcase and cut it into little pieces," she vowed, spying the turnoff for which she had been searching the past ten miles. "Down the road a bit, my eye." The last pithy comment was aimed at the gas station attendant who had given her directions to reach Blackwell's ranch.

There were other qualified people in her profession, and this article certainly wasn't her usual cup of tea, a fact she had vehemently pointed out to Daryl. She had refused to act as substitute, pleading exhaustion. Then Irene had begun her campaign to find Jade a man. Since Irene had agreed to marry Daryl she had gone from staunch loner to marriage advocate. After enduring two blind dates in three nights of staying with her friends, Jade had decided Daryl's favor was a godsend. Until now!

A moment later she swore sharply. Jade's muttered epithet coincided with a dinosaur-size bump that rattled every tooth in her head. Clenching her jaw, she ignored the bumpy road and stepped on the accelerator. At this point she didn't care if she broke an axle or bent a tire rim into a corkscrew. She was going to reach Russell Blackwell's ranch before another hour passed or her contrary car was going to expire in the attempt.

Swirls of rock dust billowed behind her as she fishtailed toward her destination. The appearance of a house on a small hill, surrounded and shaded by trees, was a beautiful sight. The smooth arches, delicate creamy-pink stucco and wide windows sheltered beneath a terra-cotta-tiled roof, whispered of Florida's Spanish heritage. The barbed wire fence that had edged the road gave way to white-railed paddocks. Buildings popped up in some of the enclosures.

Decreasing speed, Jade turned into the parking area to the left of the house. Silence filled the car when she cut the engine. Nothing moved, neither animal, person, nor even a gentle breeze in the pines. Absorbing the peace and the sudden coolness beneath the trees, Jade sat still, refreshing herself. She had made it. Her gaze wandered over the scene, her artistic eye cataloging a dozen or more photographs: the play of light and shadows over the courtyard, the luxurious profusion of color in the rambling vines of purple and scarlet bougainvillea against the south side of the house, and the action shot of the bay mare and foal grazing in the corral to the west.

He had watched her reckless approach, a speculative look in his eyes that wasn't reflected on his face. Daryl had described her as unflappable no matter what. The portfolio the agent had sent him was impressive, as well. Her noisy arrival was not. For the most part his animals were wild. He couldn't take a chance on some hotshot writer-photographer spooking them during the next two weeks. With that thought in mind, he walked toward the cleared area at the side of the house. If she wasn't suitable he would send her back to New York. He stopped soundlessly and leaned against one of the trees shading the lot. So far she hadn't seen him. The opportunity to study her unaware was more than he hoped for. What he saw did nothing to reassure him that Worth had not foisted some glory hound on him, fancy portfolio notwithstanding.

The woman wasn't beautiful. Instead she had the subtle looks that would turn a man's head, that would intrigue and capture before a defense could be raised. The intense expression on her face told of her interest and approval of his home. That should have been a plus. She was obviously tired, hot and glad to be at the end of her journey. That should have stirred his sympathy.

None of the "shoulds" worked. One thing held his attention. The woman attracted—not appealed—to him. How could she? He had yet to speak to her. But pure man-woman chemistry made his heart beat faster in rejection of the unwanted intense reaction, which he could not tolerate. The article she had come to write and Hideaway itself was too important. The work he did was more complicated than it would first seem, and it would take all his concentration to present his story in the best possible light. His instincts told him this woman threatened that. His decision made, he spoke.

"Are you planning to spend the day in there?" The test began, one he meant to win.

Shocked at the low-voiced intrusion, Jade turned. Her eyes widened in surprise. "How did you get here?" she demanded. Usually her senses were far more alert than this. Perhaps she was even more tired than she realized.

"Walked."

Simple, brief and to the point, his answer carried no hint to his identity or his thoughts. Feeling distinctly at a disadvantage before his silent appraisal, Jade reached for the handle to get out.

"Are you expected?" the man asked, still without moving or giving any sign he cared one way or another.

Jade hesitated as her lazy senses finally tingled to life, her eyes narrowing while she studied him. Tawny hair, tanned skin, regular features and dark lashes that shielded eyes as yet an undetermined color. And last but definitely not least, a long-limbed body that somehow, even in its present seemingly relaxed stance, conveyed an alertness and leashed energy that was both unexpected and unsettling. Awareness feathered down her spine, surprising her. It had been a long time since she had reacted to a man in more than a strictly friendly way.

She glanced up to find his gaze locked on her face. His amber eyes stared at her for an instant before his lashes dipped low to hide . . . curiosity? Interest? Irritation? Denial? All of those, she was certain, yet there was also something else she couldn't define.

She had learned the art of camouflage early in her career, and she used that knowledge now. Firmly banishing her unwanted reaction to the far reaches of her mind, she leaned back and forced the tension from her body. "I'm Jade Hendricks. Daryl Worth sent me," she explained calmly. The vacation she had promised herself when this was over had just been stretched from two weeks to a month.

"You have some identification?" She was not reacting as he had expected. Most people would have gotten out of the car by now, yet she sat there. Beyond that first moment of surprise, she had been in total control. Intrigued despite himself, he watched her with more interest than before.

Jade bit back an oath at his expressionless tone, which was beginning to irritate her.

"Are we having a staring contest?" Jade inquired curiously, interested and simultaneously annoyed. The man was uncanny.

"No."

"I'm stubborn, too."

No reply.

"If you can stand there all day, I can sit here just as long." A curl of pure enjoyment shot through her, overshadowing the irritation. She sternly suppressed a grin at his tactics.

"Maybe."

I could get out of the car, she thought to herself. But that course didn't appeal to her. She didn't know why she was being challenged, but she'd find out before she left. She meant to pass this bizarre initiation Russell Blackwell had instigated. If she was certain of anything, it was her recognition of the man Irene had described as relentless as the tides and as still as the center of the night.

Russ decided to apply a hint of pressure. "If you are Hendricks, lunch is waiting in the house." She ought to give up now, he thought.

"Neat move," she commended him politely. "But I've gone hungry before." Did that lip twitch? she wondered, eyeing him intently. She forgot the oppressive heat and the assignment, and allowed the exhilaration of the challenge to fill her.

"The air conditioner's on."

"Now that's a low blow," Jade countered with an eloquent look. She had met a lot of men in her life, but this one was truly out of the ordinary. He had made her aware of him and had piqued her interest when she would rather have been irritated.

"Iced sangria in a tall glass."

Jade groaned. "I'm not going to be done in by so paltry a bribe," she shot back, barely stifling a laugh. Being amused in this case smacked too much of giving him the upper hand.

Russ openly studied her heat-flushed face. "I'll even throw in a shower before we eat." Pushing away from his resting place, he strolled toward her. She could stay... for now, he decided.

Jade was caught by the loose-limbed grace of his stride. "No wonder I didn't hear you come up," she murmured. "Most people sound like a herd of elephants in a china store."

"Do they?" His laughter surrounded them, inviting her to share his amusement. He was disappointed when she didn't. He hadn't been mistaken about the flicker of humor in those hazel eyes, but apparently she didn't intend to show it to him. "Not you, I think." Opening her car door, he started to help her out. It didn't occur to him that the gesture was old-fashioned, all he knew was that he wanted an excuse to touch her. Living close to nature had taught him the value of tactile sensations, and of when to advance and when to retreat.

Jade froze, feeling his fingers close carefully around hers. She had survived in an essentially male world for so long that she had become used to not being touched by a man even in courtesy. Many of the countries she worked and sometimes lived in frowned on contact of any kind between sexes.

Russ glanced at his hand then at her. There had been a painful memory in those eyes. "Is something wrong?"

Jade was a little angry with herself for making a problem out of so little. "No, of course not." She tried to ignore his skeptical look just as she tried to pretend she didn't like the feel of his callused hand cradling her smaller one.

Russ drew her out of the car without stepping back. Her body brushed his, her woman-scent minus the perfumes that many of her sex favored reached out to wrap around him like a gentle breeze. For an instant he had to fight the urge to really touch her. His need shocked him back into stillness.

Suddenly what he had said earlier penetrated Jade's mind. "You already knew who I was," she accused.

He nodded, watching her eyes flash. He touched a forefinger to her lips to still any more words. He could see she didn't like the gesture, but he felt that he couldn't believe she was real unless he touched her. "I knew who you were when I saw you. Worth described you well." He shrugged dismissively. The test had lost its importance. "I wanted to see what you'd do."

Flabbergasted, Jade pulled back slightly. She glared at him as he released her completely. There was a limit to her control, and he was fast reaching it. "Do you mean that little scene was a test?" she demanded as he started collecting the single duffel bag that held all her clothes, her camera cases and the car keys. The only thing he left her to carry was the shoulder tote that doubled as a handbag.

Loaded but not burdened, Russ headed up the walk. "Yes, I'm afraid so." He smiled as he pushed the front door wide with a booted foot. "It was really more of a reflex than something personal." A small lie but she wouldn't know that. "Not all people are comfortable around animals of any kind and certainly not around those that are normally known as wild and unmanageable."

His words might have been construed as an apology, but Jade instinctively knew that this was nothing more than an explanation. Mentally she shook her head over this man's ability to reduce ordinary conversation to the basic giving of information.

"But why?" she asked, hurrying to catch up with him. Now she was more curious than angry. Daryl had told her Blackwell could be difficult, but her friend hadn't mentioned he was eccentric. Russ spoke in shorthand. He had the manners of an old-world cavalier and a fluid grace she had never seen in a man. If his so-called test was anything to go by, he also had the oddest way of sizing up people.

Russ turned, his gaze traveling the length of her before settling on her face. "Worth said you were the best. Unflappable, stubborn, demanding about your work, that you had a sense of humor." He paused, frowning faintly. "I want what I'm doing here shown in an honest light. The ranch is more than just a home for the stock. Most of my animals aren't pets and they aren't tamed, only trained. They're unpredictable, especially the tigers. To get your story, you'll have to know and understand them and me. That means going where I go and to a large extent doing what I do. I had to make sure you lived up to your advance PR.''

He left unsaid Worth's strange reserve where this woman was concerned. Except for telling him that Jade was fluent in five languages, that she took some of the best pictures of anyone in her profession and that she did all of her work in some of the world's trouble spots, the agent had given him surprisingly little information. Certainly those few facts were far more sketchy than the résumés Worth had provided on the original two candidates.

"And that little charade answered your questions?" she concluded skeptically.

He inclined his head, his smile deepening. He could tell she didn't like his words. Pride and feminine arrogance were equally mixed in the look she gave him. "Some of them, or you'd be starting back to town by now." He gestured down the hall. "Come this way and I'll show you where you'll sleep."

Having no alternative, Jade found herself trailing in his wake. She couldn't be attracted to this man, she decided sternly, beginning to recognize how strongly he was affecting her. Why would she be? She hardly knew him. Maybe she needed more than a month's rest. Six weeks was beginning to sound better all the time.

Never one to run away, Jade was appalled to discover she was wishing she hadn't agreed to this assignment. She didn't like the emotions this man was generating. She didn't like feeling as though the control of her life was slipping from her fingers. She was a woman who lived by and for the moment, trusting instincts honed by her experiences to see her through any crisis. Yet here in this peaceful setting, her instincts were curiously useless.

But she had given her word. Tucking every question and odd sensation in the back of her mind, she made herself relax. Jade leaned against the door-jamb, outwardly calm. Tired or not, she could handle anything for a few weeks.

Standing just inside the cool lime-and-peach-toned bedroom, Jade watched Russ deftly place the duffel beside the bed. When he turned, she caught a fleeting glimpse of masculine interest in his eyes. It touched her, splintering her calm. She fought her excitement, reminding herself she never got involved with her subjects. How often had she told herself it was impossible to take good pictures when one was not objective. Usually the reminder was enough. This time it didn't work, at least not completely.

The challenge in his eyes was even more potent than his masculinity. She had never been able to resist a dare, although she was less reckless than her hazardous life-style might imply.

"You hardly look old enough or tough enough to have the reputation you do," Russ observed while tucking his hands into the pockets of his faded jeans. "I'm going to like getting to know you while you get to know us."

Jade wondered whether there could be a hidden meaning in his words then decided not to ask. She'd handle the situation if and when it arose. "Us?" A neutral topic was called for.

"We aren't alone here, you know. I have two friends, Emma and Sam, who live here with me. She acts as housekeeper. He's my right-hand man and a damn fine trainer." He smiled faintly, catching the flicker of surprise in her expression. "Did you think we would be?"

"To be honest I hadn't thought about it at all. There hasn't been time. Daryl buttonholed me practically the moment my plane landed. I was still in the throes of jet lag when he talked me into this." Honesty whenever possible was her motto.

Hazel eyes met amber, measuring, testing, probing for understanding and information. Then the spell was broken. "Emma will have lunch on the table in ten minutes," he offered, moving with his deceptively slow stride to the door. "That should give you enough time..." His voice trailed off as he glanced back over his shoulder with a distinctly masculine grin. "Actually you could come with me now."

Caught unprepared for the implied compliment, Jade had no rebuttal. She could only watch him leave, closing the door behind him without a sound.

"I'll be a three-humped camel," she mumbled.

Was that another test? she wondered as she dug in the overstuffed carryall for a fresh shirt and cotton push pants. Or was he making a subtle pass? she mused as she stripped and stepped into a cool shower. Soaping quickly, she examined the second possibility. Her response to him dictated she deal with the more troublesome of the two choices. So far in her career she had avoided entanglements. She kept her personal and professional lives strictly separate. Her course had been set more by convenience and necessity than some outdated code of morality. Although she shunned light affairs, she was no virgin. She had known passion, though certainly not the earthshaking variety the books spoke of with such eloquence. Maybe that was why she could find the excitement in her work rather than with a man, she thought as she got out of the shower.

A knock signaled the end of her allotted break. Casting an assessing look over her outfit, Jade was satisfied with her reflection. The rumpled, drippy image of earlier was replaced with a sleek professionalism that was her trademark. A definite improvement.

"Not bad," Russ complimented her when she opened the door. His gaze swept her from head to toe, clearly admiring the transformation.

"Practice," she countered lightly with a slight smile. She was more in control now. This was just another assignment.

"I think you were supposed to say thank you."

"Not for that lukewarm praise," she returned swiftly, eyeing him challengingly. Then she lost her detachment at the strange play of emotions that showed on Russ's face.

She was only vaguely aware of the clean, cool interior through which they passed. Stone floor, cream stucco walls and crystal lights were sheltered beneath wide, exposed beam ceilings and fluid arches.

"Well, you're not beautiful, so I can't say that." His eyes gleamed as he delivered the barb. He knew he was being outrageous, but something about this slender creature with the delicately proud carriage filled him with a reckless need to try her mettle.

"No, I'm not sure I could even be called pretty," Jade agreed easily, undisturbed by the provocative remark. Her life dealt in truth not illusion. She studied him as they paused on the threshold of the dining room. "Being ordinary has many advantages in my line of work. Not the least of which is camouflage."

Now put that in your pipe and smoke it, you outspoken male, she commanded silently.

"Lady, you're about as ordinary as a rose in a daisy patch." Shaking his head over her seemingly erroneous self-impression, he guided her to a chair. "Cosmetic-box looks fade, but pride, strength, nerve and courage last forever." He touched the shiny swath of her hair. "I'll bet you call this plain brown, too."

Jade glanced up to find him watching her intently. Curiosity showed in his eyes. He was probing, she could feel it. Yet there was no demand or cause for offense in his interest. Instead, there was almost a dare to run a race with him, to match her mind, skill and experience against his. It was a fantasy. It had to be. No man, her more-practical side reminded her forcefully, is really like that.

"I don't understand you," she murmured, unable to prevent the words from slipping out. If they were to work together it would be better to take his measure now rather than later.

He was tempted to admit she wasn't the only one who didn't understand. She was a stranger, and yet she didn't feel like one. She looked good in his home, much as his tigers looked at home in their natural habitat. When they walked, he didn't need to shorten his stride so she could keep up. She met him as an equal without losing one ounce of her femininity. He sensed more than saw her pain, strength and wariness. She challenged, intrigued and, for the moment, completely dumbfounded him.

"Do you have to understand everything? Seems to me that would take the enjoyment out of life," he returned finally, realizing she was still waiting for an answer.

Jade frowned thoughtfully. "Yes, I think I do need to understand things from the beginning. Surprises can just as often be as unpleasant as pleasant."

Again he saw an elusive shadow of pain in her eyes. It took all his willpower not to pry where he had no rights.

"Food's coming," the housekeeper announced, bridging the silence as she entered the room. Emma smiled at Jade, her dark eyes friendly in her round face. "I hope you're not a picky eater."

Jade shook her head. "No, I can eat anything." She glanced at the loaded platter of fried chicken and smiled, liking the housekeeper on sight. "Besides, I bet nobody would turn some of that down."

Emma placed the food on the table then stretched out a hand to Jade. "Russ's manners leave a bit to be wished for. I'm Emma. Glad to have another woman around the house for a change. I'm getting tired of being outnumbered."

Russ grinned. "We may outnumber you, but it never seems to do us any good when you want something. I'm henpecked without even being married."

Jade laughed, enjoying the banter. The moments of awareness were gone. This she could handle without feeling pressured. "I don't see any scars."

Russ's eyes were alight with wicked devilry. "Maybe they're in a place where you can't see," he tossed back, taking a seat as Sam entered from the kitchen. He made the introduction of Emma's husband before Sam sat at the foot of the table.

Emma was across from Jade, her eyes twinkling merrily. "I knew I should have spanked him more as a boy." Then she bowed her head.

Surprised, it took a moment for Jade to realize that they were saying grace. Quickly joining them, she let the simple words wash over her. She had almost forgotten the custom existed. Her meals were usually eaten on the run and were frequently sketchy at best. She raised her eyes at the end of the ritual and felt the first stirrings of loneliness she'd had in a long time. The warmth of these people, their enjoyment of life and their readiness to accept her was a revelation. The exhaustion that had haunted her footsteps released a notch on its stranglehold of her body.

Emma passed her the mashed potatoes. "Don't be shy about helping yourself. If you don't beat these two to the food you won't eat."

"We're not that bad, wife," Sam muttered, glaring at her even as he loaded his plate.

Russ glanced at the huge mound of vegetables Sam had just served himself and then said to Jade, "Well, at least I'm not that bad." He noticed she was finally relaxing. Pleased without fully understanding why, he smiled at her and handed her the rolls.

Jade returned his smile and took one of the crescents, still warm from the oven. "Even if you are, I think none of us will go away hungry unless we want it that way."

Emma laughed. "That's telling him, girl. I knew you were a kindred spirit the minute I saw you." She shot the men a look that dared them to dispute her. "You two better watch your step."

Two

The meal passed quickly, and the conversation was lively. Jade started out as a stranger, but it quickly became clear that one couldn't be a stranger here for long. Emma and Sam accepted her, asking questions about her work that no one had ever asked before.

"*Why* do you do it?" This was from Emma.

Jade frowned, never really having given the matter that kind of thought. "In the beginning I suppose I enjoyed it. The travel, the excitement of stumbling onto something that no one else had seen. Now it's more of a habit in a way. It became what I do." She glanced around the table, smiling faintly. "I've always been a nomad. After my mother died, Father and I were on our own, and I learned a lot about self-sufficiency. As an ambassador's daughter I had first-hand knowledge of moving from place to place, of living and working in cultures different from my own. Settling down wouldn't have worked even if I tried."

"But it can't be easy, what you do. I saw that fact sheet your agent sent Russ. I've heard about those places on the news. They kill people there."

Just for a moment Jade remembered Jassimine and her child. Her nightmare, her regret. The wound hadn't healed even after six months. Angered at herself, Jade slammed the door on the image from the past. Recalling her friend would do no good. The past couldn't be rewritten.

Forcing herself to concentrate only on the present, she inclined her head. "Sometimes. But that isn't why I go and usually isn't what I see."

Russ had seen her pain again, but this time there was a difference. It was deeper than before, alive and clawing at her mind. For just an instant he felt her anguish. The urge to take her in his arms, to offer a shelter to replenish her strength, was overwhelming. Yet, somehow, he knew she would have rejected his sympathy. If this woman had ever leaned on anyone it had happened so long ago she had forgotten when.

"Well, it doesn't seem right. A body could get hurt wandering around those places. Couldn't you take your pictures somewhere else?" Sam asked, speaking up.

Emma glared at him. "It's her job, just like messin' with those animals is your job. You take chances, so why shouldn't she if she wants?"

Jade blinked, not expecting, or seeing the need for, a defense. Sam wasn't being demeaning, only curious. She looked at Russ, wondering how to stop the older couple from arguing.

Russ shook his head. She glanced back in time to see Sam swell up his chest.

"I do what I have to, woman. Ain't the same as taking pictures where a person could get shot. You don't see anyone pointing a gun in my direction, do you?"

Emma didn't point a gun, but she did point a finger, then added insult to injury and wagged it under his nose. "Who's the old fool who let Sultana step on his foot and break three bones? Who stuck his hand in front of Coon and got a dentist's impression of an overbite? And who, might I ask, decided to try saddling one of the buffalo so he could ride around like that guy on the commercial?"

Sam glared right back at her. "I was beefing up our list of tricks. There was no reason for Grady to get that job just because he had that old buffalo tamed to saddle. Our stock is as good as his any day of the week."

"You two cut it out. Jade is going to think she has stumbled into a bin of lunatics," Russ said with a chuckle.

Emma and Sam turned as one, ready to take him on as a team. Jade watched and realized that none of them was serious. The bond of caring was clear to see. She couldn't help comparing her own life to theirs. When was the last time she had teased anyone? When was the last time she had truly relaxed? Or eaten food, not only knowing exactly what she was eating but eating her fill because she wanted to and not because she wasn't sure when her next meal would be? The answer was too long.

"What do you say to strawberry shortcake?" Emma demanded, making a strategic withdrawal.

Jade made herself smile. She had to stop this. There was nothing to be gained by comparing her life-style to this one. She was only a visitor.

"I'd say I don't know where I'd put it," she replied honestly, trying to ignore Emma's disappointed look.

"I tell you what. Why don't I give you a ten-cent tour of the place, and you can walk off lunch. We can have the shortcake when we get back." Russ made the suggestion, seeing the plea for help that he doubted Jade was even aware she had made. For a second she had looked almost helpless, caught in a situation that anyone else would have seen as normal. What made her so unaccustomed to people, he wondered as he rose, determined to find out even if he had to ask her outright.

He and Jade walked into the yard that separated the house from the barn. "I couldn't help admiring how well maintained everything is. That can't be easy." Words were better than silence, especially silence that allowed her to feel. The emotions within were new and confusing. She needed to touch base with something familiar.

"It isn't." He glanced at her, but she wouldn't look at him. She was staring at the corrals that made up the east and west wings of the barn. "But we have help. Most of the work is done by Sam and me. We do have three high-school boys who help out in the early morning and late afternoon. And if Sam and I both have to go out on a shoot, I have two neighbors I pay to come in and stay until we return." They reached the corral where Sultana grazed. Russ propped his arms on the top rail, his booted foot on the bottom one.

"When Daryl explained your work I really expected something quite different. Foolish, I suppose. I cer-

tainly should know better.'' She also looked at the
horse as she spoke. "It's a bit unusual to meet someone who trains animals for commercial use. How did
you get started?''

Russ rested his chin on his hands, remembering the
crisis that had changed his life. "I was about to grad-
uate from high school. My parents and I were coming
back from town one night. A semi lost control and
slammed into our car. I was thrown clear, but they
weren't so lucky. Mom didn't make it, although Dad
did for a while. Sam and I had to run things here. I
grew up in a hurry especially when the bills started
mounting. I had a horse named Buck that Dad had
given me when I turned sixteen. I had trained him to
do all kinds of tricks." He looked at her, smiling
slightly. "To impress the girls, you know. Anyway,
Buck and I got quite a reputation. There was a movie
crew down here at the time and they needed extras. I
needed the money to pay Dad's hospital expenses, so
I applied. The next thing you know they were paying
me to ride Buck, as well. Made a tidy little sum, but
more importantly I discovered just how much animals are used. I was too ignorant at the time to realize
how closed the market really was, how slim the
chances of success. I just knew if I could do it once
with Buck I could do it again.''

He laughed, recalling his certainty of success. "Of
course, it didn't quite work out that way. In the beginning I busted my tail more often than I cashed a
check. But in the end Hideaway beat the odds.''

Jade listened to more than the words. She heard the
rock-hard determination in his voice and had no trouble envisioning the hardships he must have overcome.
She couldn't help but admire what he had done.

"From what Daryl told me, your animals are very much in demand."

He gestured toward the harlequin paint mare. "That's more because of them than us. Who couldn't appreciate that kind of animal? Look at the way she moves." He whistled once. The mare reared, pawing the sky, mane flying, ears flattened. Another signal and she came down, whirled on her hind legs and let out a shrill neigh.

Jade followed every movement, wishing she had her camera. The beauty of the creature was a sight to behold. "I see what you mean," she murmured in awe.

Russ caught her hand. The pleasure on her face made not touching her impossible. "I'm glad you passed my test," he teased. He knew instinctively he had to keep the conversation light. "When I heard that Daryl was sending me a replacement, I was a bit concerned. Now, I'm glad the change was necessary. I think you'll be good for Hideaway."

Jade stared at him, surprised and touched by his gesture as well as his words. "Thank you." Slowly she withdrew her hand. His touch was doing strange things to her equilibrium. Just for a moment, she had felt like stepping into his arms. The thought shocked her, mocking her efforts at subduing her awareness.

Russ leaned against the wood railing, his body as casually relaxed as it had been the whole afternoon. "You're welcome," he replied absently, more interested in watching Jade's face than listening to her words. The subtle shifts of her facial expression were the only barometers he had found to her thoughts.

"So tell me more about Hideaway," she said, needing to fill the silence.

"I'd rather talk about you."

"Me?" This time she allowed her surprise to show. "What for? Emma got the facts of my life out of me at lunch."

It hadn't taken more than a few short hours in Jade's company to realize that the woman had a finely honed technique for not parting with information. Russ wasn't going to be put off. He couldn't ask her outright what worried her, but he could create situations that would give him clues.

"You know what I mean. Tell me about yourself, not your work. What does Jade Hendricks do for relaxation?" he asked quietly, watching the frustration spark in her eyes.

Jade frowned, not liking the direction of the conversation. "I travel."

"Is that all?" She was hiding now. He didn't like it and knew he didn't have a right to care, but that didn't change the facts.

Jade swallowed her annoyance. She had caught that gleam of anticipation in Russ's eyes, and she wasn't letting him goad her into an unbridled display. He was dueling with her. His thrusts and parries were skilled and elusive. He challenged her, he intrigued her, but most of all, he unsettled her when she had never felt off balance before. Pride demanded that she not let him see his effect. Common sense and an instinct for survival helped her now.

"I'm onto your game," she warned, daring him to pretend ignorance.

Russ pushed away from his resting place, his glance locking with hers. "Good, then you can't cry foul." He gestured down the long, narrow road running between a double line of corrals. "Shall we get on with our tour?"

"Lead on, great trainer man," she commanded. She pushed her bangs off her forehead, too conscious of the heat and her weariness. She hated the weakness that lingered after her last assignment and sought to conceal it.

Russ noted her exhausted expression. "We can finish up tomorrow," he offered, cursing himself for subjecting her to the hottest part of the day when he knew she had to be tired from traveling.

Jade stopped in midstride. "What for?"

"You're hot and probably tired from the trip down—" he began.

"I've been hotter and a lot more exhausted than this and still done my job," she interrupted before she thought to curb her tongue. The aggressive, defensive sound of her response brought an angry groan to her lips. "Scratch that." She tried again. "I meant, I'm fine."

Russ folded his arms and stared at her, his gaze assessing her glistening face and heated skin. "I would think that you'd be aware of the dangers of sunstroke. Didn't you say at the table that you have been traveling for the past three days to get from that Mideast desert to here?" He paused long enough for his observations to sink in. "So you tell me what would be the intelligent thing to do with what's left of the afternoon."

Jade knew he was right, but she damned his way of putting the onus on her. "I'd like to take a dip in the pool," she decided honestly, having no real option if she wanted to avoid making a fool of herself. "And maybe laze around with something tall and cool to drink while I watch the sun set," she added for good measure. She was rewarded with a smile that reached all the way to her toes to overheat her already-warm senses.

"Now that I like," he agreed with a definite nod of approval. "How quickly can you change?"

"That depends," she parried as they turned to head back to the house.

He glanced at her, his eyes glittering teasingly. "I'll be heroic and not ask on what."

Jade laughed, unable to resist his suitably martyred expression. "You're a menace," she retaliated. "Just when I think I've got your number, you shift personalities on me. I'm not sure I can handle the image of you as an older brother."

Russ drew back, stunned at her description. "Older brother? Me?" he repeated blankly. "Like hell. The last thing I want to be is a relative of yours."

"Cramps your style, does it?" she countered cheerfully, enjoying his scowl. She couldn't control a ripple of pleasure at having scored first in their subtle game of one-upmanship.

"You should be locked up," Russ declared, accurately reading her triumphant grin and its cause.

"Are you going to cry foul?" she asked interestedly, her head tipped in silent challenge.

Studying her thoughtfully, Russ slowed his leisurely pace. The expectant, hopeful look in Jade's eyes dared and enticed him simultaneously. His every instinct told him this woman was special. He didn't know how, exactly, but she had touched him with more depth than anyone had in a long time.

"Russ?" Jade prompted when he didn't answer.

"I won't cry foul," he murmured finally. "I have a feeling it wouldn't help me if I did."

Jade was puzzled at the depth of emotion she de-
tected in his words. She got a fleeting impression of
self-disgust and resignation before their path took
them off the smooth dirt track to a lesser-traveled,
bumpy route. She stumbled, caught herself, then
lurched off balance into Russ. A sharp pain sliced
through her when she landed awkwardly on her left
foot. She gasped as Russ's arms closed around her,
securely anchoring her to his muscled frame.

"Are you all right?" he demanded, his breath fanning across her temple.

Jade bit her lip against the throb in her foot while
she leaned against him. "Not exactly," she admitted
as soon as she got control of her voice enough not to
betray how much she was hurting.

Russ eased her away, his hands curled supportively
around her shoulders. "Jade, you're white as a sheet.
What the devil have you done to yourself? Where are
you hurt?"

"My foot." She closed her eyes against another
wave of pain, only to open them again. "Put me
down," she commanded on finding herself cradled
with surprising comfort against his chest.

"As soon as we get home. In the meantime you can
tell me why a simple stumble makes you look ago-
nized."

"I injured myself a few weeks ago," she murmured
evasively while trying to ignore the feel of his strength
wrapping her in a protective embrace. The heat and
the energy he was expending to carry her created a
dual assault on her vulnerable senses, ensnaring her
with the scent and touch of him.

"How?" he demanded, his breathing roughening
slightly as he neared his destination. He glanced down

at the woman in his arms, aware of her resistance and equally sure he would pry at least one answer out of her about her past experiences. "Was it on one of your assignments?"

For a split second Jade debated trying another vague response, but a swift peek at his expression changed her mind. He looked ready to drag the truth out of her if necessary.

"Yes," she admitted reluctantly.

Russ inhaled sharply, hating the possibilities that filled his mind. "How?" he snapped, unaccountably filled with rage at the thoughts filtering into his consciousness.

"Good grief! What happened?"

Jade was relieved by Emma's opportune arrival. She knew Russ wasn't satisfied, nor would he leave things as they were, but at least she had a brief respite.

"I twisted my ankle on the road," she explained while Emma trotted to keep up with Russ's long strides as he entered the house.

"I'll get an ice pack," the housekeeper decided, hurrying off.

"No, I don't..." Jade began, wishing she'd remembered that ice was the first thing she would need if she really had turned her ankle.

"Let her go," Russ commanded, shouldering open the guest room door. "It'll give her something to do, and it'll definitely take away any swelling." He knelt gently on the bed to lay her lightly in the center of it. Holding her trapped between the soft mattress and his body, he stared into her troubled eyes. "You don't like letting people help you, do you?"

"It isn't that," she mumbled, barely aware that somehow he had understood the depth of her independent nature.

Russ's eyes narrowed on her obvious sincerity. Easing away, he sank down beside her and reached for her foot. Carefully working the lace-up shoe off, he removed her socks to reveal an ugly, puckered slash three quarters of the way across her instep. Tensing, he fought the realization of what he saw. Nothing could shield him from the knowledge of the pain she must have suffered.

"Damnation," he swore, glancing up to her taut face. "And were you going to work with this? Does Worth know?"

Jade sighed at his anger. Between the throbbing of the newly healed wound and Russ's unmistakably possessive attitude, she was fast developing a headache. "Yes and no, in that order." She stared at him, daring him to say anything more.

Russ held her look, reading the challenge and the fierce heart of this strange creature. He'd seen enough scars in his time to recognize what he was looking at. Whatever had pierced her skin had left a deep gash and had contaminated the area, leaving an infection behind. Although it was obvious the infection was gone, the wound was still tender. He knew from personal experience how weak such an area could be.

"He wasn't much of a doctor." He wanted to say more but didn't dare. Jade's reserve had weakened, but he knew better than to expect her to remain off balance for long. One wrong word and she'd retreat, leaving him nothing but that professional expression he was coming to dislike.

"He wasn't a doctor at all. Just a man who cared enough about life, any life, including that of a nosy, light-skinned woman who had cost him his wife. He stitched it and kept me safe from the rebels hunting me. He must have hated the air I breathed, but he nursed me through the fever and later got me back to the city." Feeling drained, Jade leaned back and closed her eyes. She didn't want to see Russ's reaction to her story. Not now...maybe not ever.

"Here it is," Emma announced, entering with an ice pack in her hand. "What on earth!" she exclaimed on catching sight of the exposed scar.

Russ shook his head, silencing her with the gesture. "I think we'll need a hot wrap for this," he suggested quietly.

Emma nodded sympathetically. "In a jiffy." She left as quickly as she had come.

"Jade, I'm sorry," Russ apologized softly, aware of the effort she had made to answer the questions he really had no right to ask.

She opened her eyes to find him watching her closely. "What for?"

"For prying into your life. You don't owe me any explanations."

"No, I don't," she agreed. "I wasn't evading you out of contrariness." Jade was unsure why she apologized, but she did know she didn't regret her words.

Russ cradled her foot in his palm. "It must have hurt a lot." He raised his head, wishing he could steal the pain that coursed through her now and from the memory of how and where it had happened. This need to protect and heal was not new to him, but usually the focus was on his animals. Something about Jade touched him, made him aware of a vulnerability he doubted she would admit to.

"I was told I screamed loud enough to bring the soldiers down on my head," she murmured, more to herself than to him.

"It never pays to relive the past," Russ said softly, giving in to the need to pull her back to the present.

Jade blinked then focused on his face. There was understanding, sympathy and compassion in his eyes. She had expected none of them. The art of sharing had been missing in her life for so long that she had forgotten what it was like to have someone offer comfort. For one second she allowed herself the luxury of feeling. Then she felt tears sting her eyes. Her next breath came in a rush as she stiffened against the warmth and softness stealing over her. Being soft made you vulnerable. Being vulnerable got you hurt, in more ways than one. She couldn't allow it. She traveled alone.

"Don't be kind to me," she said.

Russ stared at her, hardly believing his ears. He had heard many things come from a woman's lips, but never this. "Why not?"

If Jade hadn't been so tired she never would have said something so guaranteed to raise a person's curiosity. She had intended to avoid explanations, not make more of them.

"Here it is," Emma said, returning with the hot wrap.

Again, Jade breathed a carefully concealed sigh of relief at the interruption, hoping Russ would not pursue his probing with the housekeeper in the room. She would be more on her guard from now on. She had to remember he was nothing more than an assignment.

"Lean back," Emma instructed. She tucked a pillow under Jade's foot and then laid the hot wrap carefully over the swollen area.

Jade bit back a moan, having no chance to prepare herself for the warm application. Russ was beside her in an instant to lift the pad. "Hang in there. We'll go slower this time."

"I'm sorry, dear," Emma apologized, visibly upset at her clumsiness. "I didn't realize it was so sore."

"It's all right," Jade said as she tried to ignore the pain.

"Okay now?" Russ asked.

"Fine." She closed her eyes, savoring the silence, which was marked only by the faint whisper of Russ's breathing and Emma's quiet exit.

Minutes passed as neither spoke. Jade sensed Russ watching her, but she was too tired to care. Now she needed rest. She had pushed herself for too long and too hard. Muscle by muscle, her body gave up its resistance to its hurt and she relaxed, feeling as though she were floating on a cloud. Sleep crept over her before she could stop it.

Russ sat still, his gaze focused on the slumbering woman. With her defenses down he could see the vulnerable delicacy that existed alongside her strength. Dark lashes sprayed across her softly molded cheekbones, her golden skin was as smooth and soft as the finest kid while her hair cascaded in fine waves. In repose she looked innocent. Yet those lovely, expressive eyes held too much knowledge, too many painful memories. There was tragedy and disillusionment there. This woman had seen it, recorded it and been changed by it. Her innocence should have been dead, but it was not. It was dormant, asleep as surely as Jade herself.

"Damn," he whispered, wondering how she could touch him so. He wanted to hold her in his arms, shield her from all that she had known. A stranger. A woman he had not even known existed a few hours before. His feelings were crazy, but they were real. He stirred restlessly. Her hand slipped from her stomach to the bed. The soft palm, the slightly callused fingers that were half curled like a child's, looked so defenseless.

"Calluses," he murmured. His mouth barely moved to form the words. "A few hours, Jade, and I care that you have work-toughened hands." He lightly stroked one finger then drew back before he woke her. She needed rest. It was time to leave.

Three

Jade drifted slowly awake, her senses stirring languidly to life. Stretching gingerly, she tested her foot for pain. Most of the soreness was gone.

"Easy."

His voice whispered out of the slightly darkened room to still her movements. "Russ?" she questioned, opening her eyes to find him standing at the end of the bed.

"I was just about to check the heat pack." Coming toward her, his concerned gaze roamed her face. He didn't tell her he had been in and out of her bedroom most of the afternoon. Her deep sleep had worried him. No one he knew slept like that unless they were utterly exhausted. "How are you feeling?"

"Better," she murmured, offering him a small smile. "Have I been sleeping long?"

"A couple of hours. I stayed with you the first part so I could change the pad." Glancing away from the curiosity in her expression, he stared out of the window. The sun was just barely peeking above the horizon as it prepared to mark the finish of another day. It was better to watch it than her face. His mind was filled with questions that he couldn't ask.

"You didn't have to," she said quietly, wondering at the faint hostility emanating from him.

"I know, but I wanted to be sure you were all right."

"It's just a scratch," she pointed out, surprised to find she needed to reassure him. "The bullet didn't hit me, only the wall. A chip of concrete did the rest."

Russ swung around, his eyes blazing at her matter-of-fact acceptance of the wound. "Damn it, woman, you could have died from that scratch," he said irritably. The risks she took had plagued him all afternoon, making it almost impossible for him to concentrate. Unlike Jade, he took safety in his work very seriously. "Have you got some death wish or something?"

Jade inhaled sharply at the unexpected attack. "So we've come to that." She pushed her body up and swung her legs off the side of the bed. If they were going to have an argument, she wouldn't be lying down like some submissive houri.

"It always amazes me that people feel obliged to point out how dangerous my profession can be. I don't tell you how to do your work, but you feel you can tell me how to do mine." Rising, she carefully eased her weight onto her damaged foot. "Don't you think it a little ludicrous for you to preach to me? Your work is no walk through the park. I don't know if I'd be brave

enough to handle tigers and other assorted wild creatures bare-handed, trained or not. Didn't you tell me
that harlequin paint tried to trample her last owner?
Who broke her of that bad habit? There's an old saying that people in glass houses shouldn't throw
stones."

Russ felt the sting of her words like a slap in the
face. "Damn you, woman," he said, clenching his
hands. "I explained how I got into this business.
Didn't you listen to anything I said? There is no comparison between my work and yours."

Jade heard the outrage in his voice, but she also de-
tected the hurt rippling beneath the surface. In an instant her mind cooled as she acknowledged her own
form of prejudice in delivering her retaliation.

"That was unfair," she admitted finally. "I did listen, and I admire what you're doing. It takes a lot of
vision and courage to turn a failing ranch around in
the kind of economy we've had the last decade or so.
To lose your mother in that wreck and to take on all
those debts and expenses of your father's injuries had
to be tough for someone just out of high school. To
create a growing concern that not only provides a good
living for you and this place, but also a home for an
odd assortment of creatures, deserves respect. You can
and should be proud of your work. There aren't that
many animal handlers in the country with your reputation.

"But what I do is equally important." She had
never tried to justify herself to anyone but her father
and that had ended in disaster. He had never understood her job. Accepted it, yes, because she was his
daughter and he loved her. But understood it, no. "I
don't run hell-bent for leather for the fun of it. I don't

deny there's a certain element of excitement in the danger, but I'm no masochist locked into a suicide course. I believe in what I do, and I'm good at it. I apologize to no one for that."

"Yes, but what about the rest of your life, provided, of course, you survive long enough to have one?" He hated waste, human or animal. Was any story, newsworthy or not, worth a life?

Jade met his eyes with unflinching directness. "You really have no right to ask that," she pointed out finally.

She was right. He was way out of line and he had no excuse for his behavior. Taking hold of his temper, he took a deep breath. "You're right. I don't. Maybe I've worked so long with animals I've forgotten how to talk to anyone."

As apologies went this was blunt, but it got the job done. Jade admired him for his ability to back off. What she couldn't figure out was what had started him on the subject of her job.

"Why don't we just forget we ever had this conversation," she suggested after a moment.

Russ inclined his head, surprised she would let him off so easily. "I don't think you should be putting any weight on that foot tonight," he began before he thought.

Jade gestured, dismissing his concern as she took a few experimental steps. "I'm fine, although I will admit I'm starving." She headed for the door. "What's for supper?"

Russ followed her, bemused at her quick change of priorities. "Emma left a tray of lasagna in the refrigerator," he replied, his gaze on the enticing sway of Jade's hips as she walked. The woman ought to be illegal. Her clothes were rumpled from sleep. She had a soft, drowsy look that gave him all kinds of very dangerous ideas, and what was worse, she seemed totally unaware of her effect on him. She took no pains to attract and that in itself was the biggest turn-on of all. She was completely natural.

"This is going to be a long fourteen days," he muttered to himself as he entered the kitchen a step behind the object of his thoughts.

"Why?" Jade asked, unable to resist the question. She knew he hadn't meant for her to hear.

Russ gave her a quelling look. "Just sit down and I'll get the food hot," he said, having no intention of answering her. He had already made enough of a fool of himself.

Jade studied him for a moment. He wasn't evading the question, he was ignoring it. It was clear she'd not get anymore out of him if she probed any further. Curious, she mused while taking the seat he indicated.

"So tell me more about your animals," Jade said when they sat down to Emma's Italian meal.

Stars winking overhead provided a delicate web of tiny lights illuminating the patio and their table. A faint breeze teased the pines. The soft glow from the hurricane lamp in the center of the table flickered over him, highlighting his sleek frame and golden hair. The night had an aura of romance but their conversation showed none of its influence.

"There's Oscar, the gator, Robber, the raccoon, Sultana, the paint, Smiley, the possum, Monarch and Kismet, the tigers," he enumerated. The inhabitants of Hideaway were visually famous but few cared about their real names. Animals who were used by name in commercials or shows were few compared to the many that served in various capacities.

"Stop," Jade ordered, holding up her hand to cease the role call. "Daryl said you wanted more than just a PR release. Give me something I can get my teeth into. Stories of what the different animals do and how. The crazy things, the funny little slipups that would appeal to the reader. I know you want a serious account of your work, but it's always good to add a little smile occasionally."

She had a point, Russ realized as he took a sip of wine. He had given a lot of thought to the kind of story he would prefer done. Until now he had resisted telling the story behind Hideaway. He had trusted Daryl to find the right person to do the job.

"The best place to start would be with Oscar," he decided, choosing one of the oldest residents of his ranch. A neutral topic suddenly seemed a good idea. "He was the second critter I was given. Before he came to us, he had been a neighborhood's unofficial pet from the time he was a baby. Hand-fed with table scraps, he had lost his fear of man. Then one day he wasn't little anymore. No one wanted to face his full set of teeth to feed him his dinner. Oscar didn't know he was no longer cute. All he knew was that his food supply had dried up. He got irritable and very annoyed with his so-called friends." Russ shrugged. "You can guess how the good people felt about that. 'Take him away. Cage him up before he hurts someone.' The only problem with that little scenario was who wanted a hand-raised, tough-skinned set of teeth on four legs? No takers. 'Then let's put the creature down.'"

The anger he had felt at Oscar's plight, as well as the animals he had not been called on to rescue, thickened his voice with disgust. "Fortunately for Oscar, we did want him. He gets his table scraps and then some, here. He repays us with reasonable obedience when he's in the mood." He smiled at her surprise. "All the creatures here aren't tamed by any means. Most of them were born wild. They are unpredictable and potentially dangerous.

"I think that's one of the things I find the most difficult to get across to the kids when I speak at the schools and clubs. You'd be surprised how often Oscar's story is repeated without such kind results. People buy or catch baby possums, raccoons or birds then try to make them into pets like the family dog. It doesn't work. The coon and the possum sprout teeth that would make a shark envious. The pet becomes dangerous and is gotten rid of as quickly as possible."

Jade studied him as he spoke, liking the dedication in his eyes, the impassioned defense he presented. There were so many uncaring people in the world. It was nice to find dedication in any form. That caring attitude had to be threaded through the article. The anger he controlled and directed to make a difference in a situation most people took for granted would be the fire needed to bring the piece above the level of ordinary.

"You mentioned schools. What exactly do you do?" she probed, wanting to hear more. Not just for the assignment but for herself, as well.

"I give a series of talks around the county when I'm between jobs. The program is designed to educate kids to the dangers of handling undomesticated animals and, of course, there's a great deal of emphasis placed on the ecology and man's role in the balance. I have most of my animals because someone intruded on their habitat, so I have practical examples to use when I speak.''

"Are you telling me you take Oscar with you?''

"No, but I do take Coon and Smiley along with one of the baby coons and possums that always seem to be around here. There's nothing like holding a tiny ball of fur in one hand and then showing a caged adult complete with razor-sharp teeth and claws. No one looks into a possum's mouth and comes away unimpressed with his ability to protect himself.''

Jade nodded, easily picturing what he meant. She was impressed with this man. The drive that it had taken to establish Russ in his field was tremendous. Yet he had not rested when he had made a name for himself as others had done. Instead he had taken his animals' diverse histories to heart, striving to educate the local public and now, with this article, to reach out to a wider audience.

"You should write a book,'' she murmured, thinking aloud. She could almost envision the finished product. It would be dynamite.

"I've thought about it,'' Russ admitted, concealing his surprise at her words. He had told no one of his idea as yet. It was odd that this globe-trotting woman, to whom his story probably seemed like tame stuff, would mention his dream.

"So tell me about this book you want to write,'' Jade invited.

Russ shrugged. "There's not much to tell. It's just an idea I don't really have the time for, though sometimes I wish I did. That and the talent.'' He frowned, staring at his glass of wine. "I envy people like you who can put words on paper. It took me years to finish college."

Startled by the irrelevant piece of information, Jade didn't speak for a moment. "You mean you went to a university?" she asked before she thought.

He glanced at her in surprise. "Of course I did." The frown deepened into a scowl then cleared. "Oh, I see. You thought I never continued on after high school."

"It was an honest mistake," she defended herself.

He chuckled, reaching out to take her hand. "It was. But let me tell you about Emma and Sam. Neither one of them would let me shirk the college bit. My parents had set aside money for it and I was going. It took me six years to complete four, but we did it."

The pride in his voice for the people who had helped fill the place left empty by his parents' deaths was unmistakable.

"Well, if they helped you manage that then a book should be a snap," she replied, a little envious of his family unit. She and her father loved each other, but it was the kind of love that thrived with each having their own freedom. She had never regretted their attitude until now.

"I hardly think it would be a snap. My talents are definitely not in that direction, and I'm not even sure the book would have merit. The last thing I would want is for it to be published and then sit on the shelves unread. If it is written I want it to mean something."

Now she understood. Hideaway and its work was so important to him that he was unwilling to risk just anyone to tell its tale, himself included.

"Perhaps Daryl can help you locate someone when the time is right," she suggested carefully. If she hadn't been doing the kind of free-lance work she did, the idea of tackling Russ's project would have caught her fancy.

Russ met her eyes. She would give him an honest opinion, he was sure. Why shouldn't he ask her? "Do you think it has merit?"

Jade hesitated. Because it mattered to him she was tempted to say an enthusiastic yes, and that disturbed her. It was the first time in her life she considered being less than completely honest. But truth was important to her. "It might," she said slowly, choosing her words with care. "It depends on how the material is presented. But that would be true of any subject."

Russ thought that over. He had wanted an honest opinion. He had gotten it. The trouble was it didn't answer his question. "Could you do it?"

Jade's eyes widened, not expecting the offer. "I don't know. Maybe." The possibilities of his story were there. She could feel it with every well-developed instinct she had. "It's not really my field, however. Besides, I have other commitments."

"Commitments that can't be broken? I thought you worked for yourself. When Daryl explained his role in the setup, I thought that meant most of you picked your assignments according to your interest."

Feeling pushed, Jade pushed back. "For the most part I do. But in this case I would have to settle down in one place for a while. I don't do that. I like being on the move. I don't want or have an apartment, a pet or even plants to take care of. I like it that way. Working on a project like this would be a tie."

Russ tipped his head studying her, his expression openly skeptical. "Are you telling me you don't have a permanent address?"

She nodded, sipping her wine casually. His reaction was nothing out of the ordinary.

"But where do you live between jobs?"

"A hotel. Camp out. Stay with someone I know." She shrugged.

He noticed she didn't say stay *with friends*. He wondered why, even while he continued to stick to the issue at hand. For every question Jade answered, six more popped up in its place.

"What do you mean camp out?"

"Just that. A lot of the countries I visit are very primitive. It isn't so hard to live off the land when you put your mind to it. And I'm rarely alone. There's always a guide around somewhere."

Russ couldn't help but stare. "But what about friends? Your father?"

She looked at him. "What about them?"

"Don't you . . ." He stopped, knowing what he had been about to say was less than tactful. "Where do you celebrate holidays?" he substituted instead.

Jade laughed softly. "Do you have any idea how many holidays there are in the world? I have seen most of them and celebrated them all. I haven't missed anything, so don't pity me."

She'd made a joke, but there was no way to disguise the edge to her voice. She didn't want Russ's pity or his disapproval. She wanted him to see her as she was, without illusions. If they were to work together, it would be easier for them both if he understood her. Then a little voice reminded her that she had never gone to such pains to explain herself. The tables had never been turned in such a way that she became the interviewee.

Russ was silent for a moment. He had probed to learn about her and realized that Jade moved through life like the wind, touching but not lingering in any one place long enough to put down roots. She liked her life and apparently wanted no other, yet something troubled her deeply. Those shadows under her eyes hadn't appeared overnight. That tense demeanor was no product of simple tiredness, and her guarded expression was so ingrained on her face that he doubted she noticed it. She awakened instincts in him that he didn't understand, but he knew no creature could stay hidden for long. Eventually, something would touch a nerve and the animal would bolt. Man or woman was no different. Whatever haunted Jade, whatever made her whisper through life without staying in any one place for long, would be revealed if he would be patient. With that thought in mind, he waited for her next move.

Four
———

"What about the tigers? How did you acquire them? I know they're an endangered species, so you couldn't have just bought them," Jade asked, wanting to change the subject.

Russ studied her, realizing her uneasiness in the abrupt way she spoke. He would have expected her to show a bit more finesse. "Actually, they're not mine in the sense of owning them. Both Monarch and Kismet are circus bred and trained. Up until three years ago, Monarch, the male, had been part of an act. Then he mated with Kismet, who incidentally didn't perform, and for some reason known only to himself, became awkward and difficult to handle. He wasn't exactly mean, just apathetic, as though he hated being separated from Kismet. His trainer was a friend of mine. He mentioned the problem he was having and how hard it was to try to remedy the situation during the season when the circus was on the road."

"So you offered to help?"

Russ shook his head. "Not exactly. Circus people handle their own trouble if they can. Besides, I didn't think I was qualified. But, in this case, nothing worked. At the end of one of the tours, the trainer and the owners decided they'd had enough. One morning I got an early call asking if I wanted the cats, complete with hands-on training during the off-season. That winter was an illuminating experience for all of us. Monarch and Kismet acted like they had come home. My friend taught me enough to handle the cats and take them through a few easy tricks. By the time he was ready to go, the owners were satisfied I'd take good care of their animals and that the cats would do better with me. There were only two stipulations. One, I could use either animal in any film work, and two, all offspring were the property of the circus.

"The money Monarch and Kismet have made over the past three years has built their quarters, paid feed bills and insurance, and I've had a little left over to expand and improve the ranch. The cats now have a much larger place to roam and far less traveling to do, and the circus has the cubs to ensure the survival of their act."

Russ was pleased with her obvious interest. It boded well for the article. "The tigers are really why I decided to try going public with an article. The more I'm around these cats, the more I want to do something with a more far-reaching effect. Until recently, I've been too caught up in just getting myself and Hideaway solvent. Now I'd like to return some of what these extraordinary creatures have given me, and I'm not just talking about the exotic animals like Monarch and Kismet. All of them, from great to small, deserve better than man has shown them. A lot of people are beginning to know there is a desperate wrong that needs to be righted, so I'm not unique or newsworthy in that sense, but the ranch and its work is. Not only do we accept unusual creatures no one wants, or for one reason or another can't keep, but we turn the animals into contributing members of the ranch. Hideaway is entirely self-supporting through a partnership of humans and beasts. I like to think we're doing something valuable here, and I hope our efforts will aid the growing environmental awareness."

It was easy to climb on his personalized soapbox with an interested audience. "You shouldn't be so easy to talk to," he murmured. He was amazed at how much more of himself he had given to Jade when he had only intended to familiarize her with Hideaway's operation. "I hadn't intended to preach to you."

Jade reached across the table to cover his hands with hers. She didn't notice that it was the first time she had touched him voluntarily. Russ did.

"It's hard to be silent when you care," she offered with quiet sincerity. "I've done my share of preaching. Sometimes it's impossible not to." Jade had seen how damaging apathy could be, and because of that she valued commitment more than most.

Russ caught her fingers in his when she would have withdrawn. "I'm tired of talking about me. Let's talk about you for a while," he probed gently.

"I thought we'd covered this ground earlier," she replied evasively.

"Do you have anyone special somewhere?"

Jade stared at him, caught by surprise. "That's what I call taking the bull by the horns," she muttered, trying to withdraw her hand from his.

Russ didn't let go. "Well, do you?" he persisted.

"Why do you want to know?" she countered, irritated when he wouldn't release her hand.

"Because I'm interested in you. And I don't poach."

Jade was silenced for a moment. She hadn't expected him to be quite so blunt.

"Well," Russ prompted when she didn't answer.

Jade glared at him, feeling cornered. "No, I'm not involved with anyone. Not that it's any of your business."

He smiled at her belligerence as he lightly stroked her hand. The quiver he felt in her fingers could have been anger or awareness. Either reaction pleased him for both meant she could not ignore him. "Good. The way you were acting you would think I was asking for your deepest secrets."

Jade's eyes widened at the comment. Could he know about the nightmares? Had she cried out in her sleep? She studied him closely. Nothing in his face gave her a clue. All she saw was that watchful expression that worried her more than his questions. She shivered, unable to stop the telltale reaction.

Russ saw the shadow clouding her expressive eyes. "I didn't mean to bring up bad memories," he said quietly.

"Bad memories?" Jade echoed, startled into displaying more vehemence than she would have liked.

Russ was puzzled at her intensity. She was far from calm, he realized. What nerve had he inadvertently struck?

Jade sighed. The last thing she wanted was for anyone to find out about her bad dreams and the reasons for them. "We all have them," she murmured with what she hoped was casual indifference. The faint narrowing of his eyes sent her plunging into an explanation of how she got started in the business. If he wanted to know more of her then she would fill him with facts that would cloud the issue of her current life-style.

"As I told you, my father is in the diplomatic service. Although I graduated from college here in the States, we traveled a great deal. I got my first camera for Christmas when I was ten, and I took it with me everywhere. I sent pictures to everyone I knew, and with all the places we lived, that was some mailing list. My friends enjoyed them and were always begging for more, so one roll of film and one small instamatic soon grew into a special lens and an SLR camera—single lens reflex," she added, clarifying the initials automatically.

"Then there were books and a fluke much like your own. The father of one of my high-school friends was an editor for a top English travel magazine. He saw some of my photos and bought them for a story. I was sixteen and sheltered enough not to realize the obstacles ahead when I decided to become a professional photographer. I can't honestly say I ever envisioned doing what I am now." She shrugged, dismissing the long-ago dreams of glamour work and artistic experimentation.

"How did you end up globe-trotting while hunting out revolutions, riots and wars?"

"I was in the right place at the right time or the wrong one at the wrong time, depending on your point of view."

"Elaborate," he commanded insistently. He recognized what she was doing but went along with it anyway. She wasn't giving him the facts he really wanted but only pieces of her life.

Slightly diverted by the return of his verbal shorthand, Jade peered at him through her lashes, a tiny smile playing at the corners of her mouth. "I thought I'd broken you of the habit of one-word communication," she teased, beginning to relax. A small yawn took her by surprise. The wine was beginning to get to her.

Russ shook his head, his expression warning her. "Jade."

The soft ripple of her name on his lips sounded like a caress. Despite the faint edge of authority in his tone, there was an unmistakable coaxing quality in his drawling voice. And it was to that more than the demanding side that she responded.

"The magazine I worked for at the time handled a wide variety of material. I was only one of their people on the scene when a surprise, bloodless coup toppled the government of—" she produced the name of a much-publicized country with a dramatic flair, enjoying his amazement.

"That article, plus my other work experience, led to a call from an international news service. I stayed with them until I went free-lance two years ago." She started to lean back in her chair before she remembered Russ still held her hand. Wiggling it experimentally, she unsuccessfully sought her release. If anything his fingers enclosed hers more securely as he gazed at her.

Finally, Russ asked the question that had been plaguing him since midway of her recital. "Are you satisfied, or would you change something?"

"Two months ago I would have said I was happy with what I've accomplished. I've made a name for myself. I'm fairly well-off." She paused, wondering how to explain. The vague suspicion that she was being uncharacteristically open slipped in and out of her mind. Her irritation was gone as though it had never been. Somehow Russ had made it easy for her to talk about herself. Puzzled, Jade looked at him. She couldn't tell what he was thinking. His hand was warm on hers, the calluses rubbing lightly over her skin.

Russ watched the emotions touching her face. He was surprised at her uncharacteristic openness and candor. No other person he knew would have been so honest about their lives without displaying at least a bit of pride. Yet Jade had stated her achievements with an intriguing matter-of-fact attitude. It was almost as if she believed her success was little more than an accepted reward for diligent work. No more, no less.

"I guess my only regret is not having any special tie to one person or even a place," she admitted at last. She had said so much she might as well finish. "Recently I've started to miss that." She grinned, suddenly needing to dispel the now-somber mood. "Besides, Daryl insists I find somewhere on this planet to hang my hat. He says he's too old to get ulcers trying to find me when he has an assignment." She blinked, feeling as though she were trying to look into the sun. Exhaustion was catching up with her.

"I can see his point," Russ agreed dryly, refusing to be distracted. He was beginning to recognize Jade's tactics. When he got too close to her innermost thoughts or the subject became too serious, she was ready to shift the conversation. Although her maneuvers frequently frustrated his attempts to learn more of her, the ability and finesse she displayed intrigued him. He started to tell her he was onto her little game, then changed his mind as he saw her stifle a small yawn.

"Tired?"

Jade nodded. The wine she had consumed, coupled with the peace of the outdoor setting, had made it difficult to resist giving in to her exhaustion. Even the stimulation of their conversation was losing its hold on her.

Rising, Russ drew her up with him. "Then it's off to bed with you," he decided easily. The chase was no challenge when the quarry was too tired to run. He would wait for tomorrow.

"But what about the dishes? I can't let..." The rest of her protest was muffled by the touch of his forefinger to her lips.

"You can and you will leave them to me. I'm domesticated and housebroken." He stared into her sleepy eyes, fighting a battle with himself. She was all soft and drowsy. And he was a man. Desire simmered under his control, heated by the way she leaned into him. She was dead on her feet, and he wanted her. Her voice was husky with fatigue, making him want to scoop her into his arms and carry her to his bed.

"What the devil...?" he breathed as she began to rest more of her weight on him. Bending slightly, he swung her up, smiling at the startled surprise in her eyes. "Don't argue, woman. Just lie back and accept my limited services or you might not wind up in your own bed—" he paused, grinning down at her "—alone."

Jade touched his cheek. "I'd be poor company tonight," she mumbled, nestling her head into the warm cradle of his shoulder. She was barely aware of speaking.

Russ dropped a kiss on her temple, determinedly ignoring the feel of her soft body in his arms. He wasn't fool enough to believe she was aware of what she had just offered. "Honey, I think if all I did was hold you all night, I'd be happy," he whispered against her hair as he headed down the hall to the guest room.

"What a lovely compliment," Jade replied, allowing her eyes to succumb to the weight urging them to close. The security of Russ's embrace wrapped her in a lighter-than-air cloud of contentment. The click of the door as he nudged it shut barely impinged on her consciousness. She opened her eyes briefly as he lowered her to the turned-down bed.

"Do you want this thing off?" he asked, referring to her caftan.

The question slipped out of the deep shadows to touch her gently. "No, it's very comfortable to sleep in," she murmured huskily.

"I should leave, then," he said, making no effort to do so. Every part of his body was tight with the denial of the temptation before him. Desire without appeasement was no easy burden for a man to carry.

"Yes, six o'clock comes early."

Drawn to her softness and cloaked in the intimate haven of darkness, Russ lowered his mouth to the enticing shape of her slightly parted lips. One taste, he promised himself as he touched them lightly. The feel of her indrawn breath of pleasure made him ease away.

How innocent she looks, he thought as he gently cupped her cheek in his palm. And how fragile. She doesn't look like either an international photographer or a self-sufficient modern lady, but only like a lovely, desirable woman. Her eyes clouded with passion as she held his gaze. He had seen her fire once in a brief flash, but now he had a glimpse of the heaven of her femininity. She was woman, a quintessential creature to stir his senses to madness.

"Sleep well," he whispered, backing away while he watched her. To stay one more instant was to risk his control.

Jade gazed at him, knowing he desired her. It would have been easy to hold out her arms, to call him into her bed. Yet she did not even though her body ached for a physical release. She was here to do a job—to tell Russ's story. She could not allow herself to forget that.

"You, too," she murmured.

For a long moment they looked at each other. Then, with a sigh, Russ turned and left the room. Jade lay awake for a short time after he had gone. It wasn't in her nature to brood once a decision was made, but this time she could not stifle a feeling of regret. Finally, her eyes closed and she slept.

The next morning, Jade was surprisingly rested. There hadn't been a hint of the nightmare that had plagued her for months. Buoyed by the freedom she felt from the haunting memory, she found herself humming as she showered and dressed. She might not be able to carry a tune in a bathtub, but this morning she didn't care. After collecting her camera and some extra film, she followed the delicious scent of fresh-brewed coffee to the kitchen.

Emma glanced up with a smile as Jade entered. "I hope you're going to tell me you like a big break-fast," she greeted Jade, barely pausing in the act of slipping a pancake onto a big stack already filling the platter on the counter.

Jade eyed the golden circles liberally dotted with yellow fruit. "These smell heavenly, but what are they?" she asked. It had been a long time since she had felt as if she had a home. But here in this busy room, warm with the heat of the stove, Jade found a contentment that was alien to her.

"Pineapple pancakes. My specialty," Emma replied promptly.

"And my favorite," Russ announced, coming through the back door just in time to add his bit to the conversation.

Jade swung around, her lips curving in a faint smile. It was impossible not to smile on a morning like this one.

"I thought you promised to wake me."

Russ shrugged, his eyes gleaming with laughter. "Nothing could have gotten through to you over your snoring."

"Russ!" Emma's startled exclamation echoed her husband's as he trailed Russ into the room.

"I can't help it if you have a weak voice," Jade countered with deceptive sweetness, diving right into the fray. She couldn't have Russ as a lover, but she could enjoy his company.

"Weak?" Russ's brows rose in astonishment while his friends chuckled in delight at Jade's swift parry. "Grant me strength," he muttered, taking his chair at the round table.

"See, even you agree," Jade teased, sitting down next to him. Accepting a platter of fried eggs from Emma, she placed them in the center of the table.

Pouring each of them a cup of coffee from the pot at his elbow, Russ mumbled, "That's only an expression, not an admission of guilt." Keeping his eyes firmly on Jade's expressive ones, he tried to block out Emma's and Sam's appreciative looks.

Jade wondered what had gotten into her. She hadn't felt this young, this uninhibited in a long time. In some ways it seemed like forever. What magic spell had Russ wrought to make her feel and act like a carefree spirit on the threshold of discovery? She couldn't remember the last time she had felt safe enough to indulge in a frivolous bit of play.

Safe?

The word flashed in her mind, taking hold. It was true, she realized with sudden insight. There was a peace and serenity about Russ's home that created a special barrier between her and the stark realities of the past. Russ himself seemed touched by the same gentle quality, yet there was strength in him, too. This was no tame creature, no pet for a woman to keep, but a predator who had chosen to be kind, who purred when he just as easily could have bitten.

"Earth to Jade," Russ whispered against her ear. Touching her shoulder lightly as she started, he noticed the shadows in her eyes. He felt anger well up in him at her dark memories. He hated to see any creature with pain in its eyes. That it should be this fragile-looking woman hurt him in ways he didn't understand and wasn't sure he wanted to recognize.

"I'm here," she answered with a smile. She had never shared with anyone the ugliness she had recorded, seen and lived. She had decided long ago that the pictures she took and the words she wrote would be the weapons with which she'd fight cruelty. But nothing would ever induce her to share her personal tragedies, even if it meant she carried nightmares with her the rest of her life.

Russ studied her, unable to believe the swift recovery she had made. One moment she had been hurting. Now he saw nothing in her expression but the peace and enjoyment of a new day.

Jade noticed his probing look. He was trying to understand her, so she tucked herself away from him, remembering all the reasons why she couldn't be as open as he wanted.

"Bring on the pineapple specialty," she commanded, deciding a diversion was needed.

"Coming right up," Emma shot back with mock servitude, an attitude greeted with a crack of laughter from her spouse.

"Don't get her started, you two," Sam warned, ducking agilely as a pot holder sailed at his head.

"This is a crazy house," Russ pronounced, slipping four cakes, two eggs and six pieces of bacon onto his plate in quick succession.

Jade eyed his swift movements with awe. "I'm glad you let me get first choice."

Russ looked up to point at Sam. "That's why."

Jade followed his gesture to find Sam making a large dent in the laden plates. "Good Lord," she breathed. "Where does he put it all?" Sam's frame was reed slim and wiry.

"I think he's got a hollow leg," Emma offered, copying Jade's more-modest servings.

"Nope. Russ just works me to the bone," the older man supplied between bites. "And what he doesn't take out of me, those critters of his do."

Jade got to see the truth of Sam's words a short time later as Russ, with her his shadow, began the first of his chores for the day. "So you feed the stock before you have your own breakfast," she said, tucking facts into mental notes for writing up that evening.

Russ nodded as he led the vividly marked harlequin paint horse toward a small schooling ring. "I've mentioned the high-school boys who help us. They feed and water the two buffalo, the dogs and the horses, clean the kennels and muck out the stalls while Sam and I take care of Oscar, the tigers, the raccoons and possums. We usually finish about the same time. The guys leave and Sam and I come in for breakfast. After that we exercise the animals that need it and work on new tricks, or 'behaviors,' as we prefer to call them, until after lunch. Of course, there's always some kind of crisis, either major or otherwise. Vet visits, animal fights, equipment repair, not to mention the daily maintenance that, in many ways, is just as important as the health of the animals. Then there's the upkeep of the property itself." He frowned, wondering if he'd remembered everything.

"That kind of schedule makes me tired just thinking about it," Jade confessed. It was impossible not to admire the work Russ did.

Russ halted at the enclosure's gate and couldn't help but stare at Jade. For a second the sunlight glinted off her hair. Despite the job at hand, he allowed himself to hold the picture of her questioning eyes and the alertness of her expression. She was so lovely yet so very capable. He blinked, dispelling the sweet warmth of his senses.

"I thought I'd put Sultana through her paces. Hopefully you'll get some good shots. Then, during the next few days we'll do the same with the rest of my menagerie, plus whatever else you can think of worth photographing."

Jade found no fault with his plan. "Let's do it," she agreed, stepping back to lean against the corral rails as he opened the gate. She readied her camera without taking her eyes from Russ and the horse he led. Calculating distance, assessing the background possibilities and light exposure, she was quickly lost in the world of recreating images. Light, shadow, lines, angles and curves flitted through her mind as she watched the action unfold in the clearing.

Silhouetted against a cerulean sky, a rearing mare, mane flying like a banner, nostrils dilated with effort, muscles tight with the strain of the powerful pose, was caught at the instant of perfection. She finished one roll and reloaded quickly. A shot became lost because the sun flirted with a cloud and cast a shadow that Jade didn't want. Another was gained out of a muffed trick. Russ's gentle smile, more eloquent than a dozen pictures, told of his caring for the animals in his charge.

By the time Russ led Sultana out of the ring, Jade's knees were dusty from kneeling in odd positions to achieve just the right angle. Her cheeks bore more than one smudge. She was hot and sticky but satisfied with the material she had gotten.

"She's fantastic," Jade exclaimed softly as she joined man and beast. Giving Sultana's damp black-and-white neck a pat, she smiled at Russ. "You two look great together. And thanks for wearing that scarlet shirt and those black jeans. It made a fabulous contrast."

A grin lighted up Russ's face. "Believe it or not, it was Emma's suggestion. She was ready to murder me this morning when I appeared in my usual denims."

Imagining the scene, Jade chuckled. "Got you scurrying back to redeem yourself, did she?" she teased.

"In a heartbeat." He turned away to lead Sultana back to the barn for a well-earned rubdown. "The things I do for you two."

"And for your animals." She couldn't help being pleased that, even for one small moment, she was part of a family, of a way of life that was both productive and caring. It was a harmless pretense. No one would lose as long as she remembered that tomorrow and goodbye waited around the corner. She could enjoy herself as long as she didn't play for keeps.

Five

——

Jade marveled at the way the following days settled into a comfortable pattern without leaving her prey to the restlessness that had become her companion. She rose early, breakfasted with Russ and his friends, and was then ready to shadow Russ. Rolls of exposed film matching the notes she added to her journal each evening accumulated rapidly. She'd learned firsthand about the unpredictability of the wild. One day she'd seen the pair of tigers perform like docile house cats, the next they were sullen, doing nothing but glaring at anyone who came near.

Many of her shots were lost through a wrong movement by the animal Russ was working, making her even more aware of how complicated his job was.

Yet Russ never seemed to lose his temper. He would calmly repeat his command until she could get the shot she needed. She'd nod when she was satisfied, and he would reward her with a smile for her perseverance. Recognizing that, in many ways, this facet of their relationship was similar to that of his rapport with his charges, she should have been mildly offended. Yet she wasn't, for there was too much respect for her work and opinions in his attitude. He made no secret that he wanted the photographs depicting the use of animals to be as comprehensive as possible. Sparing neither his time nor effort, he gave her every support, right down to organizing a darkroom for her use with a local photographer.

Jade glanced at the stack of prints in protective envelopes on the car seat beside her. Russ would be pleased with the latest results of their work, she decided, a tiny smile curving her lips. She was delighted with them herself. The thought of the book they had talked about that first evening returned to mind. Her smile changed to an expression of concentration as she considered the possibility more fully. The pictures she had taken were too numerous for the current assignment, but she hadn't been able to resist the extra work. So many of the shots were worthy of public viewing. She was saddened to think they would never be seen unless Russ decided to do the book.

A bone-jarring bump reminded Jade to pay attention to her driving.

"Damn road," she swore. "I'll be black-and-blue by the time I leave here." She'd been up and down the bruising drive more times than she wanted to recall. "Anything beyond one trip is more than one human should endure," she added irritably when her left front wheel dropped into a deep crevice. Gunning the motor a bit, she powered up and out. Using every curse in every language she knew, she played dodge 'em with the craters for the rest of the drive.

Russ watched her stop in a puff of dust and a screech of brakes. "One of these days you're not going to stop in time, and Sam and I will be replanting Emma's flower bed." He grinned as he walked toward her.

Gathering her photographs, extra film and handbag, Jade slipped out of the door he opened for her. "And if you'd have that blasted cow path graded, I wouldn't have to negotiate it with a prayer and a kamikaze's handbook for a map," she returned swiftly. She studied him, seeing something in his expression that hadn't been there before she'd left. "Okay, give," she commanded, recognizing an eager anticipation too pronounced to be focused on the pictures she held.

Amazed at her perception, Russ stared at her. "How did you know? Sam didn't stop by Hanley's and tell you when he went into town, did he?"

"Sam? What's he got to do with this?" Jade asked, surprised in turn. "I haven't seen him today. I left right after breakfast while you two were still down at the buffalo pen with the vet."

Reaching over, Russ plucked the bag of newly purchased film from her overloaded grasp and urged her up the front walk. "We've got a shoot for a men's cologne commercial with Monarch. In Atlanta in a few days."

"You're kidding," she exclaimed, catching some of his excitement. As quickly as it had come, her smile died on remembering which animal was named Monarch. "You can't be serious. That tiger is a monster. He tried to take a swipe at you the day you worked with Sultana," she protested vigorously.

She had faced bullets, knives, terrorists and madmen bent on conquering the world, but watching Russ work the big cat in an open arena, with nothing between him and claws and teeth, had sent chills down her spine. He was a trained professional who didn't take stupid chances, but the knowledge hadn't made any difference. The tiger hadn't behaved well, in fact, he had looked as though he were doing more than contemplating mischief. There was real intent in those metallic yellow eyes.

"I told you 'trained,' not 'tamed,' remember? Monarch's been in front of a camera and audiences dozens of times without an accident. He's healthy and he knows what's expected of him. I'm not saying he'll be perfect," Russ reassured her, watching her expression. He was well aware of Jade's concern over the big cat. The knowledge that she cared about him even this much pleased him—not that she'd ever admit it. She was still determined to hold him at arm's length, and so far he had let her set the pace. But things were about to change.

Jade followed him down the hall to his den, her senses blind to the restful blue, nutmeg and cream room. "I'm not talking guarantees, either," she denied, taking a seat on the overstuffed sofa. "But I heard you and Sam talking yesterday. You said it might be time to retire Monarch and Kismet."

Sitting beside her, Russ stretched his legs as he studied her worried face. "Do you think I'd endanger myself or anyone else to Monarch's power? Or the animal himself? Haven't you learned more about me than that?"

He spoke the words but his mind was more taken with her changing facial expressions. Jade was so

caught up in her concern she wasn't guarding herself
as carefully as usual. His breath quickened. The chase
was drawing to a close. She was growing accustomed
to him and the life he led. He had wanted that, had
worked to achieve it, but he wasn't fool enough to let
his desire for Jade push him into taking her knowing
that there were only a few days for them to share. He
wasn't made for temporary pleasures, temporary lives
and beautiful globe-trotters, no matter how much his
body might find her appealing. Wanting Jade had
made him take a chance that even now he wasn't certain would pay off. He frowned. He had been trying
to ignore his attraction for too long.

"Of course, I don't think so," she disagreed impa-
tiently, thinking she had hurt him in some way.
"Maybe it's my intuition, but that tiger worries me. I
saw his eyes when you worked him." Suddenly remembering the photos she held, she upended the en-
velope on the low table in front of her. Trying to
convince him of the gamble he was taking, she shuf-
fled carelessly through the stack to extract four color
prints. Thrusting them at him without glancing at the
vivid images still etched in her mind, she spoke
sharply, "Look at those and tell me what you see."

Russ gazed at her for a second before focusing on
the photos. He'd become familiar with her work during the past couple of days, but he still couldn't help
being impressed with her ability to capture her subjects. Monarch's orange, black and white hide seemed
to shine as though the sunlight had been captured in
each gleaming strand. The power and grace of the
huge jungle cat flowed in every muscle as the animal
stood poised on its hind legs, front paws lifted over his
head. Then there was a close-up of the beast, its enig-

matic face tipped, hypnotic eyes gleaming above a mouth drawn wide in a mighty roar. Another photo showed Monarch lying down, and another was an action frame of his leap through the air, caught the instant his huge hind quarters thrust him into space. His beauty, savagery, gentleness and power were all there.

"These are superb," Russ said, looking at them one more time.

"I know. You two are good subjects," Jade agreed, realizing he hadn't seen any of what she had tried to show him. She leaned over to look at the photos before tapping the first one with a forefinger. "That's what I want you to see. My camera doesn't record what isn't there. Look at that tiger's expression, Russ. It's mean. Monarch isn't playing."

Russ studied the photograph, beginning to realize what she meant. "I've seen him appear angrier," he commented, glancing up in time to catch the disappointment in her eyes. "I've already decided this will be the cat's last assignment. He's earned his retirement, and his temperament is growing more unpredictable every year. We've been fortunate he's worked for us this long. I don't take unnecessary risks." He held up a hand when she would have interrupted. "And no, I'm not unusually concerned about this job. There's no reason to believe everything won't go like clockwork. It's not even going to be a particularly complicated shoot. It's just a small vignette for a new men's cologne. Monarch walks with the hero into a clearing where a beautiful woman lies in wait, etc., etc."

Thinking over his description of the action involved, Jade found some of her anxiety ebbing. She wanted to believe she was overreacting. "It doesn't sound too bad," she admitted slowly, feeling something niggle at her mind. She remembered too many times when her instincts had kept her out of trouble. There was a piece missing, she was certain, but what was it?

Russ laid the photos on the table before turning to her. "Now that we've taken care of that, how would you like to go along? It'll mean postponing your return to New York for a while. Are you interested?" He put the proposition to her, counting on her interest to gain him a few more days.

Jade went still as his words washed over her. So far she had won the fight with her increasing need for Russ. She'd struggled with the peace and quiet energy of both the man and the ranch. She hadn't realized that she had forgotten about her upcoming return to New York. Now she was being given an opportunity that she would have jumped at in other circumstances. Her hesitation spoke of how strong Russ's influence was on her. Only to herself would she admit that she didn't know if she could survive anymore exposure to the man. When there was respect, liking and admiration it was almost impossible to ignore attraction. It was beyond her not to see and want to know Russ more intimately. She wanted his hands on her body, stroking her with the gentleness he gave his animals. She wanted to taste him, to feel him fill her, driving out the emptiness she hadn't known existed until she came to stay at Hideaway. For the first time in her life she admitted she was afraid her choices were being taken from her. She looked into his eyes and saw emotions she did not know how to cope with. He was a man created to build, to stay. She was the wind, slipping across the land, touching but not lingering long enough to be still.

Jade stared at him. Could she refuse? Her work had to be served. She had never given her profession less than full measure. It was her pride and her responsibility.

"It would certainly add to the article," she admitted reluctantly.

Russ heard something in her voice that was new, and she looked uncertain, vulnerable. He leaned closer, driven by the need to touch her. His finger slipped down her cheek. "Is that the only reason?"

Jade wanted to pull away but couldn't. The look in his eyes held her in place, demanding the truth she didn't want to give. "No." The word was soft, husky, filled with the emotions she had been trying to bury.

He smiled at the admission. Finally. He had waited, day after day, watching for a break in the wall of professionalism that had hidden her from him. "I'm glad."

Jade moved then. His smile did what her willpower could not. "Well, I'm not." She rose from the sofa as though it were a hot seat. "I don't want to feel like this." In her agitation she didn't guard her words. "I don't do this."

Russ watched her pace. "Do what, Jade?"

Jade swung around, glaring at him. It wasn't fair he could look so relaxed. She felt backed into a corner, and he was acting as if he didn't know what they were talking about. "I don't get involved with my subjects. I told you that in the beginning. It's this place. All of you." Her eyes narrowed. "It's not supposed to be like this."

He wanted to grin but couldn't for she would never understand. She was so rattled. "How is it supposed to be?" He was goading her, but he needed to know what she was thinking and feeling. He was tired of pretending that she was just another woman, that he didn't want to take her to bed with an ache that was slowly tearing him apart. He wanted to bury himself in her, pull down those walls so that not even a thought could separate them.

Jade started to speak, then stopped. Taking a deep breath, she strived for calm. Russ was on his feet in an instant. He would not allow her to hide from him again.

"Don't you dare," he commanded, catching her by the shoulders. "I'm tired of both of us pussyfooting around as though we don't know we want each other. I hurt and I think you do, too. Face it and me." He challenged her, he taunted her and trapped her. He didn't care what it took, but he wanted what they were feeling out in the open.

"I don't know what you're talking about." For the first time in her life, Jade took refuge in a lie.

Russ ignored the words and took the mouth that uttered them. Jade had no chance to protest or evade him. He filled her senses as he wrapped her in his arms and took what she tried not to give. Russ felt her resistance—and the passion that was just barely within her control. Had the first existed without the second he would have let her go. He was no man to take what had to be forced. So, instead he gentled her with his hands until her body yielded, flowing like silk within his grasp. Differences, needs and the future faded as the fire licked upward, encircling them in its ring of heat and light.

"You're a witch," Russ whispered, pulling her deep into the cradle of his thighs. Unmindful of his power, he held her tight, wishing he could absorb her into his being.

Jade lifted her head, her lashes weighted by the desire filling her body. Her legs trembled. "We can't—"

His mouth swallowed the rest of her words. "Don't deny us," he demanded against her lips. He lifted her high in his arms and carried her to the couch. Laying her down, he half covered her with his length. "Neither of us have anyone. We can take this loving for this moment."

She shook her head. "You don't know what you ask."

His hand cupped her breast, teasing the nipple lightly. He smiled as he felt the tremor that rippled through her. "I know. Believe me, I know."

Jade stared into his eyes and saw what she had refused to see for these long days: determination and the ability to beat the odds, to risk and survive to risk again. This was a man who could stand before wild animals with only a word and a touch to protect himself. He could carve a job and a life out of the land and with the creatures who walked it. But more than that, for a moment, he could still the wind with a whisper.

"Share today with me, Jade." His words were no plea. Rather, they were a command for her to grab her courage in one hand and take his hand in the other.

"You win," she whispered, offering him her lips.

Bending his head, he covered her lips in a brief, possessive kiss, stealing her breath and then returning it with some of his own. Jade moaned softly, feeling her control slip farther away. Nearly dizzy with want-

ing him, she arched beneath him. Russ slipped his
fingers to the buttons of her blouse. The cotton came
away leaving behind a scrap of lace and silk. Budding
nipples poked through the thin fabric, begging to be
touched. Jade gasped as Russ teased the erect peaks.
Her hands pulled at his shirt, baring his muscled torso.
She inhaled deeply, drowning in his scent.

"Beautiful, creamy skin," Russ whispered as he
began a trail of kisses over her throat to the edge of her
bra.

The slow, moist caress drove Jade wild with wanting. She twisted beneath him, needing more than this
love play. "Russ, please."

He lifted his head, his eyes glittering with passion.
"I will please, I promise." He released the bra and
stripped it from her body in one smooth motion. Her
jeans and his followed almost as quickly.

Jade groaned as she rose up to meet him. Her hands
tightened on his shoulders, binding him to her with
every ounce of strength she possessed. "You're beautiful," she said with a sigh. His muscles rippled with
power and grace beneath her touch.

When his tongue flicked out to caress one nipple,
she stiffened in unbearable tension. She could feel her
breasts swell. She whimpered in pleasure, reveling in
the look in his eyes as he gazed at her.

"That's it, honey, burn for me. Tell me you like
what I do for you."

But she had no words, only primitive sounds, she
thought, lost in a sensual haze. Russ was touching her
in ways so new, she had no defenses. She could only
entreat with her body as she tried to return his offered

pleasure. She felt him shudder as her hand closed around the shaft of life created for her completion.

"So good," he groaned. He lifted his head, his amber eyes demanding she return his look. "Don't stop."

Her hand tightened, and he arched as a quiver coursed through every muscle in his body. And then he claimed her softness, and his fingers began a rhythmic pattern until the center of her being tightened and convulsed. She was writhing beneath his manipulations, and she gasped for air. She instinctively tried to close her thighs to capture and hold those maddening instruments of torture that were slowly driving her to the edge of insanity.

"No, not yet," he groaned, staring into her face.

He moved his touch and she suddenly cried out, her body bowing in that ancient offering of woman, as an indescribable sensation shot through her. "So responsive." His hand moved again. "And so fantastically soft. Are you ready for me?"

Never had so few words been so welcome. Ready? She was an incendiary bomb waiting to explode. His mouth covered hers, his tongue invading the eager opening at the moment he joined them as one in a powerful surge. Hesitating for an instant, he allowed her to adjust to the feel of his body. Then he began moving in the primitive melody that succeeded in satisfying one need while creating a feverishly new one.

Jade had the sensation of falling off the edge of the world into a dazzling place of sheer pleasure. The hot words he breathed in an erotic litany in her ear were almost as arousing as his driving urgency.

The tension mounted toward the final explosion of sensation. Eagerly she rose to meet each bold thrust.

Russ closed his eyes in an agony of pleasure. It filled her with satisfaction to know it was the enjoyment of her body that brought him this exquisite torment. That every movement of her hips, every touch of her hand could cause this strong man to gasp and shudder with the need searing them with white-hot flames.

Her legs held him cradled to her, her fingers cupping the hard, sculptured curve of his buttocks. He felt so good. Faster...deeper she strove to race him to the peak they sought. Then it was there. She threw herself headlong at the pinnacle, suffering the impalement to achieve the soul-revitalizing rebirth. Her mate cried out as he followed.

Jade was vaguely conscious in that moment of dazed euphoria of Russ shifting positions to lie beside her, enfolding her in the warm shelter of his arms. He tucked her head into the hollow of his shoulder, where she could feel the thunder of his heart beneath her ear and see the light mist of perspiration on his sun-burnished skin. Her tongue darted out in lazy curiosity to taste the supple smoothness of his shoulder. It was slightly salty and deliciously exciting even in this moment of complete contentment.

Russ found her actions stimulating, and his thundering heartbeat accelerated beneath her ear. He drew a deep breath that was more a shudder. "Don't do that, honey," he groaned, his arms tightening around her. "At least give me a chance to recover a bit."

"Why? I might miss something," Jade whispered provocatively, brushing her head back and forth like a cat on a favorite cushion.

She could feel a chuckle ripple through his body as he pushed back the hair on her forehead. "Believe me,

I've no intention of leaving out one thing or losing one moment of our time. I promise,'' he vowed as he lifted her chin with his forefinger. His lips covered hers in a kiss that echoed the depth of need in his words.

Six

***

Russ sucked in his breath when Jade strolled through the sliding glass doors. The intense desire tightening his muscles had increased rather than eased with the possession of Jade's body.

Sunlight embraced her slender form, painting a golden glow over her bare limbs and spotlighting the brief, beige, mesh swimsuit she wore. Technically, the garment was a one-piece affair, but in truth it was little more than four strategically placed scraps of fabric joined by an almost-invisible webbing. A fire was lit deep in his gut. Images of her naked body, hot and passionate in his arms, flashed through his mind. As she drew nearer, he became mesmerized by the deep glitter of feminine satisfaction in her eyes. She knew what he was thinking, and she made no secret of the pleasure she found in his arousal.

"Don't you dare look at me with that mysterious little smile," he warned when she stopped a few inches away. "You wore that thing on purpose." His statement wasn't really an accusation at all. He liked knowing that Jade felt free enough with him to revel in her femininity.

Jade nodded, her lips widening in unconcealed delight at his reaction. "After yesterday, last night and this morning, I figured it was time for a little spice," she teased. "So far, you've seduced me by moonlight and dawn, with flowers and candlelight and, last but not least, during a game of hide-and-seek in the barn. Now it's my turn." Lifting her fingertips to his chest, she delicately ran them through his dark gold chest hair. A deep shudder rewarded each of her tiny caresses.

"I didn't seduce you," Russ returned, encircling her wrists in a reflexive need to stop her exquisite torment. What a woman she was. Unashamedly honest about her desire, she still retained the softness of her femininity.

"True," she breathed, dropping a kiss at the base of his throat. Arching into him, she nudged him closer to the pool's edge. "I'm glad it's Saturday."

"So am I," he agreed, hardly hearing the seeming irrelevance. Instead, he was drowning in the heat of her touch.

"Emma and Sam said to tell you they'd see you early Monday."

"Monday?" Russ gripped her waist, her words finally penetrating the passionate web she was spinning.

Jade lifted her lashes, her eyes filled with the force of her need. "They've gone to the coast for the weekend. Sam said to tell you Kyle will see to the animals until he gets back.'' She wondered if he'd accept his friends' blatant, though well-meaning, interference. For herself, she was delighted with the time alone with Russ.

Russ recognized the hesitancy in her expression and the ripple of tension invading her body. ''You want this, don't you?'' He had to know what she was thinking. Now.

As little as two days ago, Jade would have retreated from the question. Today she met it and him head-on. ''Yes. I do want to be with you. More than I can tell you.'' She hesitated, then plunged ahead. He had given her so much, taught her things that she hadn't known existed. ''I want to stop the clocks for a while.''

Russ heard more than the words. Still the gypsy, the wanderer. This was only a rest to her. He knew she cared because she wasn't a woman to lightly give her body, but it wasn't enough. Anger surged through him. He forced it down. She had been honest with him at great cost to herself. He would still wait and work. The future was ever changing, and he was a patient man. The chase was not yet over.

''We can't stop the clocks, but we can steal time,'' he whispered, cradling her face in his hands. The deeply buried fear in her eyes cut through him. She hadn't expected him to take what she offered. ''Emma and Sam's idea is just what I wanted, too. Much as I care about them I want to be with just you.''

Jade closed her eyes and felt almost weak with relief. For just an instant she had thought he would be angry at the older couple's tactics. ''I'm glad,'' she murmured, touching his lips with a kiss.

"Sometimes I feel like we're trying to crush days into minutes. We're racing an unforgiving clock. I can't stop but neither can you. For whatever reason, we are here, in this place, together. I may die a little when our time is done, but I want you to know I would do it again if I had the chance." Facing him, she offered him the only reassurance she had. She never made promises.

"If I live to be a hundred, I won't forget this moment," he murmured huskily, his fingers gently tracing her face. Would she ever stop surprising him with her strength? She gave without seeming to, absorbing hurt and returning it transformed by the beauty of her touch and her honesty. She was clothed in sunlight and tears, yet he never saw her cry. Her eyes sometimes held the fiery darkness of hell itself, but she never gave less than gentleness, compassion and tenderness.

Words demanded more than either of them had to give. Their bodies spoke the only language that could exist in the fusing of their worlds. Russ covered her lips with his as he lifted her in his arms. She came to him willingly, generously. For a fleeting instant, he wondered how he would live with her memory when she left. Could he let her go? Could he smile and send her back into the flames of Hades, knowing that dangers and ugliness awaited her in the harsh, unmerciful darkness? She had told him much about her life, but he could tell there was more she never mentioned. These were the nightmares that woke him in the center of the night. These were the images that drenched her body in sweat and brought the tears she would not shed in the sunlight to her eyes. He wanted to protect her, and he could not. He could not cage her when she wanted to be free. Some creatures died in captivity.

Tightening his hold on her, he carefully descended the steps into the pool. For now she was here, safe in his arms. He hadn't lost yet.

"Russ?" Jade whispered, feeling tension invade his body. In their time together she had learned him well. It wasn't passion with which he embraced her, nor was it need. Could he be feeling the sands in the hourglass slipping away? Was he, too, counting the hours?

"Promise me something?" She spoke impulsively, from a need to still the hand of time.

He glanced down at her as he stood waist deep in the warm water. "Anything," he agreed.

"Pretend there is no tomorrow."

Russ lowered her to her feet, her breasts pressed against his chest. She had asked the one thing that was beyond his power to give. "You have learned to live in the moment. I have not. I believe in tomorrows and stability and a place of my own. Don't ask me for what I can't give. Just as I take you as you are, don't ask me to be less than I am."

Jade closed her eyes on a wave of pain. Happiness always had a dark side. Nothing in her life had ever come without a price. "I never meant to hurt you," she whispered.

He framed her face with his palms. "Look at me." He waited until she opened her lashes. The tears he had only seen in the dark were now in the sunlight. And these tears were for him. "Like you, I don't regret what we share. Given a choice I would still take these days with you."

The tears overflowed in a silent stream of truth and grief. Jade wrapped her arms around him, holding him with all her strength. No words passed her lips as she lifted herself to him. Russ took her with a fierceness he had never known. He had no pride, no tenderness. She matched his need, driving him to reach beyond himself in an effort to give more. His body said all that he would not. Jade answered in the only language she knew. He took her to the heights of ecstasy in an aquatic mating more exciting than a fire storm. Jade slipped back to earth in his arms, her body floating languidly beside his on the wide pool steps.

"Did I hurt you?" Russ asked, lightly cupping the full curve of her breast.

Jade shook her head, smiling. "Your hands couldn't hurt me. When you make love to me, I feel beautiful and more rare than a goddess. How could I be hurt by that?" She would have warmth and laughter if she had to fashion it out of dreams and fantasies. Curling an arm around his neck, she drew his head down until their lips almost touched. "I still owe you one seduction," she purred throatily, visually caressing the cleanly sculpted planes and hollows of his face.

He raised his head to smile. "Seduce away, honey. I'm all yours."

"Where did you learn to cook like this?" Russ asked while Jade served him a second helping of chicken cacciatore. It was nearly midnight, and the moon was bright in a star-studded sky. All around them the earth seemed to sleep as they sat amid the courtyard flowers and dined.

"Italy."

Grimacing at her brief, unenlightening response, he probed for more information. "Where in Italy?" One day she would give him a complete answer on the first question.

Jade passed him his plate, a smile lurking behind her considering expression. She knew her one-word replies drove him nearly as wild as his did her. His insatiable curiosity about her had yet to wane nor had hers about him. "I'll trade you. You tell me how you got that jagged scar on your hip, and I'll tell you about my crash course in Italian cuisine."

"You're extremely good at blackmail," he pointed out, "and evading my questions."

Jade lifted her wineglass, her eyes meeting his across the candlelit table. "A regular Jade of all trades," she parried. His reaction was astoundingly swift as he tensed, golden desire staring back at her in a blink.

"That's cheating," he breathed hoarsely, downing his Lambrusco in one swallow.

"You think so?" Jade tipped her head, vainly trying to ignore her own response. Maybe she'd been crazy to try to redirect his interest this way. Yet she didn't want him to discover what she had been doing in Italy that summer. "I rather thought you liked this," she added, continuing on the path she had chosen.

Russ put his glass down and rose, his gaze never leaving hers. She thought she had fooled him with her subtle change of mood, but he had learned too much about her now. Certainly more than Jade seemed to realize. Since Jade had awakened in his arms from her nightmare of Jassimine, she had changed. She had shared her pain and grief in the darkness with an openness that had moved him. But when dawn came, she once more became the reserved woman she had always been where the danger of her job was concerned. She seemed determined to spare him and, because he didn't want to hurt her, he let her play the role the way she wanted.

"Come on woman, I need to hold you," he commanded, gathering her to him.

Though she had become accustomed to his lightning response, Jade was unprepared as he lifted her from her chair and into his arms. "Russ?" she murmured when she tucked her head beneath his chin.

He grinned at her, wicked lights dancing in his eyes. "I've decided to collect another seduction. I got one yesterday and I want one tonight while we're still alone. Tomorrow Sam and Emma return, and the day after that we leave for Atlanta." He entered the house barely watching his steps as he made his way to the master bedroom.

"You're so good at sweeping me off my feet," Jade said, laughing softly as he lowered her onto the spread.

"And you're so sexy to hold." Working swiftly he untied the straps at the back of her neck to release the cream-and-aqua gown. Cool air whispered across his chest when Jade returned the favor by unbuttoning his shirt. He caught her smile as he shuddered in reaction when she teased him with light strokes. "You're going to wear me out," he warned, undressing.

Jade shook her head, her hair brushing his bare stomach with tantalizing delicacy. "Can't. This is the gift that keeps on giving, and I am a greedy creature." Reaching up she pulled him down to her. "I'm storing up every second in my memory." Just for an unguarded second, the desperation she felt shone through her words.

Russ cradled her close. His eyes darkened with his own need to hoard images, in case tomorrow was as black as Jade feared. "I love making memories with you," he said huskily. "We've made a small mountain of them already, but let's try for Mount Everest this time."

Hazel eyes met amber in perfect accord. The solitary weekend was almost over. The future neither of them spoke of was looming nearer with each breath they took. For two days they had enjoyed themselves and the passion they shared.

"Let's climb the peak," Jade invited with a soft sigh. "Last one there is a slowpoke."

Russ laughed as he knew she wanted him to, before dipping his head to taste her lips and drown himself in her softness.

The moon raced across the sky, a mute spectator of the couple entwined on snowy linen. Twin cries of fulfillment were carried on the night breeze to fade in the darkness. Then there was silence as the sunrise crept relentlessly toward the horizon. Pale, ghostly fingers parted the night, slicing the velvet cocoon of the fantasy world they had created with harsh realities. That which had been was now only a cherished memory.

Jade awoke first, disturbed by the light piercing her slumber. Easing carefully from Russ's embrace, she padded to the window to stare out across the eastern quarter of Hideaway. The room that had been a haven all weekend was closing in around her. Restlessness was nipping at her heels. The morning breeze teased her face, reminding her that the horizon was close and the land beyond it unexplored. A sigh rose deep from her soul. It was almost time to be on her way. She glanced over her shoulder, her gaze resting on her lover. Part of her wanted to stay and that alone was a surprise. But the wish wasn't strong enough to destroy the urge to leave. To stay was to settle, to know each day as she knew her own face. To go was to discover, to meet the day armed only with herself, her intelligence and her courage.

But there was another side to her wanderings. The loneliness, the emptiness of her life without someone to share with, the darkness of the night spent in some godforsaken corner of the world where no one would mourn her passing. She shuddered, wrapping her arms around herself. Standing at the window, looking over Russ's small kingdom, she realized she was irrevocably changed. She would never again see just the horizon and the sun beyond. Shadows waited to darken the way, clouds gathered and hung from the sky to blot the light. Solitude became a curse.

Russ watched her through his lashes. He had felt her slip from his arms and resisted the need to hold her captive. She was restless, pacing the room the way his big cats paced the confines of their cages. His body held hers, but her mind, her heart and her soul yearned for freedom. The confusion in her face, the faint frown between her brows told of the cost she was paying for their loving. He realized that on some level she wanted to stay, but that it wasn't enough. She turned back to the window. Head up, eyes alert, her gaze roamed the view as though she could see forever. Even her slender body seemed poised, ready to spring away at the first opportunity. And her expression! To describe it was beyond his words. There was such need written there. Pain seared him as he read what he had known all along. He saw the same pain in her face as she came back to bed. He opened his arms to receive her.

"You were awake," Jade murmured, somehow not surprised.

"I felt you go," he said simply, looking into her eyes. He traced the clean line of her jaw with his fingers. "It's almost over, isn't it."

She nodded, curling against him, for once not wanting the desire to smother the need to be held.

Russ cradled her, thinking about the woman and her background. Jade had been honest with him, and in the truth she'd given him he hadn't found one reason for her need to be completely free. No deprived family background, no love affair gone bad or a traumatic event that she had to escape. Nothing. Yet no matter how he tried he could not convince himself she wasn't running.

"I had a black mongrel once that was as smart as a whip and a good dog for just about anything. He had one flaw, though, he just wouldn't stay home. No matter how hard I worked with that mutt, he never learned where he lived. He was constantly either lost or running away, and I'd always get him and bring him back. Then one day I didn't find him soon enough. He got hit by a car before I could reach him."

He pulled her tight against his chest. He'd forgotten about Coal until this moment. He was surprised he'd even drawn the comparison. "I loved that crazy fool, but he couldn't believe in it, I guess. He ran away, probably telling himself there was something waiting for him in the next pasture."

"Do you think I'm running?" She couldn't look at him, but she had to know.

Russ sighed deeply, afraid he was right and hoping in a way he was wrong. "Yes."

"Why?" Her voice was a sharp knife cutting through their closeness.

"I've never met anyone with the capacity to care that you have. If you ever love, you'll be so defenseless that you'll hurt not only for yourself but for the one you care for. Some part of you knows that, I think, so you've chosen this way to live. You spread all that depth around, using it to help many. In the process you can distance yourself enough to survive, because those you help are really strangers. The one time you let yourself care was with Jassimine and her child and look what happened."

"My nightmares," she whispered, not wanting to believe him.

"And the vacation to the States you haven't needed in twelve years," he prompted gently. He turned her in his arms, wanting to see her face.

Jade raised her eyes to his to find a warm, golden glow of understanding. "You don't know that for sure," she argued. "I'm no coward, emotional or otherwise." She had spent her life depending on her strength. She didn't want to know it was illusion. How could she go back even thinking that?

Russ drew her close, feeling resistance where there had been pliancy. "No, I can't be sure," he agreed. "But if this is what's driving you, only you have the key. It's locked somewhere in that quick, analytical mind of yours. Look for the key, Jade." He cupped her face with his hands so that she had to look at him. This time she would not escape him. "Stop moving long enough to face yourself."

Seven

For a moment Jade relaxed against him, drawing strength from his calm. The feel of the beat of his heart against hers, his warmth holding the morning chill at bay, and his breath softly stirring her hair, were a temporary shelter from the thoughts crowding in her mind, creating chaotic images of the past. Details she had believed she'd understood took on a new dimension. Suddenly the flood of information was too much. With a stifled cry of pain and frustration, she jerked out of Russ's arms, her eyes reflecting her inner torment. It would be easy to take what he offered, but would it last? No thing, no person had ever held her in one place for long.

"I've got to be alone," she gasped, backing away from him as though he were the devil incarnate.

Seeing the haunted wildness in her gaze, Russ swore. He stepped toward her, his hands outstretched. He never took another step because Jade broke, and whirling, she ran across the room and was gone. Feeling as if he'd been kicked in the gut by a mule, Russ froze, his eyes on the door through which she'd fled. Raw, emotion-charged words ripped past his lips while he absorbed the result of his handiwork. Seconds flowed sluggishly into minutes, but he remained still until he calmed somewhat. Feeling years older, he walked slowly to the door to close it.

"I care about her, damn it," he muttered fiercely, as if that fact excused him somehow. The memory of her eyes stabbed him mercilessly until he groaned aloud. "I should have found a better way." But he was fighting for something that was becoming more important to him by the day. What had been desire was growing and changing, altering his perception of himself and his world. He wanted Jade, but he was beginning to need her in his life, as well. The combination was powerful, overriding caution and patience.

Suddenly feeling unclean, he strode to the shower, turning on the hot water to a stinging blast. Jade was strong, he reminded himself, unable to forget her animal cry of agony. Suppose she ran? The idea took root in his mind, bringing him out of the stall in a rush. Beleaguered creatures would go to ground if they got half the chance. He would allow her all the time she needed, but he wouldn't let her escape. The knowledge hammered at him as he swiftly dried and got dressed.

"I won't let her leave," he vowed, entering the hall hurriedly.

His gaze went to her door to find it open and her room empty. For a second he was sure she had bolted, then he saw the empty duffel beside the dresser and the clothes hanging in the closet. She was still here. She hadn't run. Sighing in relief, he headed toward the kitchen at a saner pace. A faint clatter of metal gave him the hint he needed as to Jade's whereabouts. He stopped just inside the doorway, his glance on her tense back as he hunted for the words to say.

"Jade." Only her name passed his lips. She turned. But he wished she hadn't when he saw her face. He had expected some show of emotion, but her expression was as clear and as calm as a lake at sunrise. No hint remained of the agony that had contorted it just a little while ago. In fact there was even a faint smile playing around her lips, although it didn't reach the placid surface of her hazel eyes. For an instant he wasn't sure whether he was glad or sorry that she could bury herself so completely. On the one hand she wasn't crying but on the other he wanted her to feel what was happening to them.

Jade hid behind the mask she had worn so much in the past when confronted with a scene she couldn't handle. She saw Russ's surprise and his careful study of her expression. She fought neither.

"Sorry about the scenario earlier," she murmured huskily. "It was the shock." An understatement if ever there was one, she added silently. Leaning back against the counter, she forced her muscles to relax. She had made enough of a fool of herself for one day. She wouldn't do it again.

"Maybe that should be my line," Russ commented quietly, moving nearer but not too close. She appeared at ease, but he could see the effort she was making to foster that impression. He had to remember she was as wild as any creature he had ever gentled.

Jade shook her head. "No, we've never been less than honest with each other. I'm glad that hasn't changed." She glanced down at the empty cup she held then back at him. "I will be equally honest and say I don't agree."

Russ stared at her. It hadn't occurred to him she would deny his words without considering them fully. Her ability to focus on an issue, to examine all the angles was one of the traits he admired most about her. Irritated, determined not to show it, he said, "Don't you think that's a little unrealistic?"

Jade shrugged, ignoring the inner voice that agreed with Russ. Catching the flash of temper in his eyes, she tensed slightly despite her best attempts to appear relaxed. "No."

Annoyance turned to anger, pushing at his self-imposed restraints. "You realize you're throwing away what we have without a backward look." He took a step closer.

Jade faced him squarely, almost welcoming the release of the emotion roiling within her. "I know I'm not going to try to live up to the image you have of me." Her chin lifted, daring him to deny her charge. "You want more than I can give."

Russ clenched his hands at his sides. Of all the ways she could have chosen to escape him this was the least expected and the most painful. "Damn you," he swore. "I'm not trying to cage you."

"Aren't you?" Jade's brows raised in mock surprise. She was hurting him with every word, yet she was hurting herself more. "It felt like that to me. You've got yourself convinced I just need someone who understands me and I'll be just like any other woman," she rushed on before he could speak. If she stopped she would regret what she was doing. "Well, you'd better think again. I...like...what...I...do." She spaced the words carefully so there could be no mistake of her meaning.

"And the nightmares? What about them? They're tearing you apart, or have you forgotten?"

Jade whitened at the reference, her control stripped away with a few words. "You have no right!"

"Right?" Russ caught her arms, holding her when she would have pushed him away. "Tell me about rights. You lie in my arms, accepting me as your lover. No restraint, no hesitation, no holding back. You're not the kind of woman who would do that unless it meant more than fulfillment of physical desire. Yet you will leave here soon, leave me—"

"Leave what, Russ? What do you offer me but an affair?" she interrupted, all but shouting at him. "Or the confinement of home and hearth?"

Russ froze at the bitterness and the pain in her words. "Confinement? Is that all you can see you little fool? Can't you see that you would be free? Can't you tell that this compulsion to roam is a trap of steel that will never release you? What happens when you're old and alone? When you can't run to the ends of the earth anymore? How will you survive then?"

Jade pulled out of his hold, hurting herself in the process. Breathing hard, she braced against the counter. "You don't know what you're talking about. You're the one who's trapped, not me. We couldn't even have two days together without arranging a small army just to care for this ranch. If we'd wanted to drive to the coast we wouldn't have been able to. All I have to take when I go is a few cameras, a duffel bag and myself."

Russ stared at her, realizing he had lost before he'd even had a chance to win this round. She would not hear him because she did not wish to. "You're so wrong, Jade." He shook his head to clear it. "And so am I. I never should have taken you. You're like the wild creatures I care for. No one can own you or even love you, for you won't allow it." He turned away from her, giving her what she said she wanted. Let her see what they had. Let her know the emptiness of being alone. He had held her in his arms, known her passion and the depth of her emotions. He was banking on those feelings now.

Jade reached out before she thought. The expression on his face drained her of the will to fight. "Russ, I—"

"Don't bother, Jade. There's nothing left to say except we made a mistake." He looked at her then. Every word tore at him. "Forget it, Jade. You were right and I was wrong. We don't have much longer. Let's finish the job you're here to do so we both are free."

It was Jade's turn to stare. He was as still and unmoving as he'd been the first moment she had seen him. The time they had spent together was gone.

The awkward moment stretched and still neither moved. The sound of a car pulling into the parking area drew Russ's attention. "That will be Sam and Emma."

Needing time to compose herself, Jade turned jerkily to the coffee percolator. Taking down three more mugs she filled them. Emma and Sam entered before she turned around. Their laughter and the recounting of their weekend made it possible for her to sit down at the table as though nothing had happened. If she didn't look at Russ or hear his voice she could almost believe the lie herself.

"Okay, you two loafers, we've got work to do," Sam announced, interrupting Jade's thoughts.

Blinking, Jade glanced up to find both men getting to their feet. "May I help?" she asked automatically.

Russ wanted to refuse but knew it would look odd if he did. So far neither Sam nor Emma had noticed the tension. "If you like." The indifference of his reply earned him a sharp look from Emma. He forced more life into his voice. "We can always use an extra pair of hands. We've got to check Monarch's cage and pack his gear. Then we'll clean him up so we'll be ready to leave first thing in the morning." To avoid looking directly at Jade he carried his mug to the sink.

Jade copied his actions, striving to behave normally. She hadn't missed Emma's curiosity. She didn't want the older couple to realize the trouble between her and Russ anymore than it appeared Russ did.

"Are we talking about washing a tiger?" she asked, attempting to work up some interest in the preparations.

Russ made the mistake of glancing over his shoulder. She was standing too close. He could see the pain and confusion in her eyes. Saying the first thing that came to mind, he widened the space between them. "And in a tub, too."

Jade stilled, her hand poised above the sink. "You're kidding, right?" Her gaze sought his, then moved away. Really looking at him hurt. The memory of his body against hers was impossible to resist when they were separated by only a few feet.

The sound of Sam and Emma's laughter was both a blessing and a curse. Three steps carried her back to the table.

"If you could see your face...." Sam chortled.

"Now Sam," Emma scolded. "Jade's reaction is perfectly logical."

It was logical, all right, Jade added silently, thinking about an entirely different response from the one Emma noted. She couldn't keep this stupidity up. Someone was bound to notice, and after only a few minutes it was wearing her out. She'd never be able to hold up until the end of the assignment. She glanced at Russ to see him watching her. They couldn't leave things as they were if they were to complete this job. She couldn't work like this—with most of her mind on the man and not the article.

Emma stood. "All of you, scat. I have work to do even if you don't."

Sam knew that tone. He headed for the door. Russ moved to Jade's side. "I'll help you get your cameras together." Emma beamed at them as Russ urged Jade from the kitchen before she could protest.

"I don't need any help, but I do need to talk to you," Jade said the moment they were out of range of Emma's hearing.

"I think we've said all we need to say. I know I did."

Jade stopped in midstride, staring at him. "You mean you want to be like this for the next few days?"

"No, I don't 'want to be like this,' as you so discreetly put it, but what other choice have you left me?" He stalked passed her. "You want to talk. Okay. Let's go to your room. It's about the best privacy we're going to get."

Jade inclined her head, knowing that being behind closed doors with him was the last thing she wanted at the moment. She walked beside him, unwillingly aware of every move he made. Even his male scent was designed to recall what she had to forget. The walk to the guest room had never been so long nor so silent.

Russ closed the door and leaned against it. Jade stood in the center of the room facing, but not looking at, him.

Jade spoke first. "We've only got a few days left. We're stuck with each other until then."

He watched her for a moment then prompted, "So?"

"What do you mean 'so'?" Puzzled, uneasy, her senses tingling with messages that confused her, Jade tried to concentrate. Something was not as it should be.

Russ sighed, raking his fingers through his hair. This was more difficult than he'd thought.

Jade stared. She had never seen him show so obvious a sign of frustration.

"Is that what you mean? We can't keep acting like this, or someone is going to suspect we're fighting."

"We're not fighting," she denied instantly.

"Then what would you call it?" He came back just as swiftly.

Jade opened her mouth then closed it.

"Right. Fighting. The point is, what do you want us to do about it?"

"Can't we go back to the beginning?" The plea was out before she could stop it. Angered at herself, Jade paced to the window and looked out. "Damn, I knew I should have stuck to my rules." Disgusted with herself, him and the whole situation, she said the first thing that popped into her mind.

"Oh just great! Now we've got an I-told-you-so. Just what we need."

Jade swung around. Anger, hurt and self-recrimination made a bad combination. "If you can't say something constructive then don't say anything at all."

Russ glared at her. "Constructive! You want constructive. How's this?"

Before Jade could move or even realize his intent, Russ had her tightly in her arms. "You came here with a job in mind—why don't you do it? I'm only a man, remember? So we had a little fun together, a little loving. Why can't you handle it, honey? You're used to running free. What's so tough this time?" He brought his lips close to hers on his last words. "Do you miss this already? Do you want me?"

Stunned at the verbal assault, Jade had no defense when he took her mouth with a punishing kiss. Then suddenly it was over and she was swaying without the support of his arms. Her lips hurt but her heart ached. The look on his face made her want to cry out in pain. "I never meant this," she tried to explain.

He laughed grimly. "Did either of us?" It was his turn to pace to the window. His back rigid with tension, he stared across the land of his home. He had to get control. He had never hurt a woman in his life, but he had wanted to hurt Jade. He needed to make her feel something, to know what she was throwing away.

"Did I hurt you?" he asked without turning around.

Jade studied his tense posture, unaware of anything but him. "No." He didn't relax. She took a step closer then stopped. "Can't we just pretend it never happened?"

He glanced over his shoulder at her, one brow raised in blatant skepticism. "Can you?"

Jade couldn't meet his eyes. The demand there was more than she wanted to see. "I wouldn't want to, but I will if it's the only way we can finish."

Fool! You did ask her, he reminded himself even as he flinched from the dispassionate words. "All right. That's what we'll do then." If she could be this determined then so could he. He moved away from the window to head for the door.

Jade lifted her head at the same moment, watching him as he brushed past her.

"I'll meet you at the barn."

Jade didn't say a word as the door shut soundlessly behind him. She simply stood there, remembering the blank look on Russ's face. Not controlled, not still, but blank, like a slate wiped clean. One moment he had been as angry and as hurting as she—then, nothing. He had locked himself away in a place she couldn't reach. Numbly, Jade began collecting her cameras. He was expecting her to carry on as though there had been nothing between them. Although it was her suggestion, she wondered now if she could do it. She had to. Whatever she felt had to be tucked away. To take it out was to open the floodgates to emotions she couldn't afford to spill. Slinging the camera case across her shoulder, she left the room. A few days and then she would be free. If she could hold on to nothing else, she still had that.

Jade left the house through the kitchen and crossed the marl clearing between the house and the barn. Entering the shadowy recesses of the stable, she paused a minute to allow her eyes to adjust to the change of light. The low murmur of voices told her that Sam and Russ were at the far end of the building. Moving quickly down the wide aisle, flanked by roomy box stalls on one side and individual tack and feed compartments on the other, she finally reached the area set aside for the various shipping paraphernalia required for the variety of animals in residence. Leg wraps, blankets, halters, tarps and the carryon cases for the smaller animals lined the walls and shelves in military precision and with hospital cleanliness.

"I know you don't keep a five-hundred-pound cat's cage in here," she remarked, keeping her voice steady and friendly. She had forced this course on them. She would follow it.

"No, it's outside," Russ explained, sounding as though they were indeed back at the beginning of her time at Hideaway. "We'll check it out after we take care of Monarch. In fact, you can help me wash it out."

Jade didn't look forward to the experience, but it was better than brooding. "All right. Lead me to it."

The three of them left the barn through the back entrance, which opened immediately into a narrow, fence-lined walkway. The path was wide enough to allow a group of animals to walk comfortably abreast. The tiger's pen was at the far end of the east side, the section that housed the more exotic of Russ's collection. A single-humped camel, a llama and a water buffalo named Dodo shared the space with a small herd of six American buffalo. All the animals had their own corrals and individual homes, but without a doubt the tigers' compound was the most heavily secured and the most-expensive single structure on the premises.

Built of concrete and block, it was a free-form design that provided the necessary access to the majestic Bengals while recreating as closely as possible the tigers' natural home. There was a small, well-fed stream running through the carefully laid out area, and a deep pool at one end. A high, strong fence surrounded the whole, allowing the human population its safety and the tigers their security from disturbance.

"You stay here until I call you, while Sam and I capture Kismet," Russ directed, all business.

Jade nodded, knowing she would be in the way when the men tried separating the female tiger from her mate. Russ had explained that although tigers were solitary by nature, they sometimes formed strong attachments with one of their own kind. Such was the case with Monarch and his lady.

Keeping her eyes on the empty clearing, Jade awaited the irritable roar that would indicate Kismet was in the small tending chute at the back of their house used for doctoring and shot giving. A moment later the expected growling rent the air followed by another deeper sound as Monarch was urged into a narrow opening leading to the training ring on the other side from where Jade stood. Jade realized that for some reason there had been a change in plans, but since Russ exhibited no concern, she relaxed.

"Okay, Jade." Russ's call was calm.

Remembering his instructions about the dangers of sudden movements, she eased down the aisle around the pen until she came to a small bench facing a ring of about forty feet. Constructed much as a circus arena, the area contained a metal pedestal and a hoop supported by slender poles. And last, but certainly not least, Russ and Monarch. The huge creature weighed close to five hundred pounds and stood nearly eight feet tall when he reared up on his hind legs, paws extended wide in a fighting stance common to his breed. His orange-and-black coat gleamed like luxurious, exotic cut velvet in the sunlight. Yet despite his glorious coloring, his movements were what fascinated Jade. Supple, delicate, they belied his size, creating a deceptive image more dangerous than any other animal. His face was beautifully expressive without the ferocity and brute strength of a lion or the cunning of the leopard. Russ's voice blended with the light morning breeze as he began to work his charge through a series of simple commands.

"Monarch! Seat!" Monarch leaped to his pedestal with ease. Jade's shutter clicked at the exact moment the massive head lifted alertly to await the next cue.

"Monarch! Down!" Another movement flawlessly executed. Another picture.

And so it went until finally Russ released the cat with the command, "Monarch! Out!"

The tiger bounded lithely through the connecting runway back to his cage. Jade stared at Russ across the empty ring, caught once again in the strange beauty of what she had seen and how Russ had directed the great animal with finesse and authority rather than fear and strength. She had seen so many kinds of courage, some flashy, some fanatical, but Russ showed her quiet, unrelenting bravery. The tiger could take him down with one swipe of one claw-extended paw. Yet Russ seemed not to notice. He had moved before the cat as though he were an overgrown tabby.

But for one sick moment Jade had noticed that look she feared in Monarch's eyes. She had lost a shot because her fingers had frozen on the camera. And then the cat had blinked and yawned and the expression had disappeared as though it were a trick of the light. What if he *had* struck out?

Jade shivered despite the heat. She had touched every inch of Russ's bronze body. To think of him hurt, scarred by the great cat, made her want to scream. Yet she had no right to even feel anything. She had forfeited that right when she had pushed him away. Her vision blurred. She did not see Russ watching her with a strange frown on his face. For one moment the blankness was gone from his eyes, replaced by the pain of her rejection. Jade blinked away the threatening tears and looked again only to find the ring empty.

Eight

I thought you were going to bathe Monarch," Jade murmured as Russ joined her. She was glad Russ had taken longer than usual to finish with the tiger. She had her emotions under control now. No more tears would be shed where she could be seen.

"I would have, but Monarch took care of that chore for us. He's been swimming this morning, and he looks as clean as Sam and I could have gotten him."

He nodded toward her camera, wishing he didn't have to play out this charade to the bitter end. For a moment he had thought he had seen tears in her eyes, but there was no sign of them now. Jade, the photographer, overshadowed Jade, the woman whom he had held in his arms only a few hours before.

Every gesture Jade made brought up images he wished he could forget. He felt as though he had known her a lifetime. The way she tilted her head, the concentration in her eyes whenever she spoke of her work, the scent of her that still lingered on his sheets and too vividly in his mind. He only had a few more days left. What if he couldn't change her mind? A fear he had never known was growing within him. He almost hated the Fates that had thrown them together.

"Did you get some more shots?"

"Yes." Jade looked away, trying to think of something to say to fill the silence. She needed words badly. "You never did finish telling me about the tigers," she murmured, hoping the subject would occupy them.

Russ was as relieved as Jade sounded. "What do you want to know?"

Jade glanced at him, trying to see him as a subject. It was impossible. Her body still carried the memory of the feel of him in her arms. "Why are they so special to you?"

"For one thing they're on the endangered species list. Do you realize how hard it is for them to reproduce out of their own element? The mother frequently rejects or even kills her young after they're born if she's not watched. So that means round-the-clock bottle-feeding, and after that the young cubs must have their sides rubbed to stimulate elimination, both of which are twenty-four-hour-a-day jobs for the first months of life. If it hadn't been for the caring of the circus people, Monarch and Kismet wouldn't be here." Russ concentrated on the tigers to blot out his emotions.

"My cats, by appearing in commercials or whatever, not only remind people who won't ever see a tiger outside a zoo that they still exist, but also the money Monarch earns allows us to continue expansion. Since we've converted the ranch to a refuge, we've handled four hundred or so assorted animals. A few, like the ones you've seen here, are permanent residents. The rest are in new homes like zoos or special animal acts. And we've personally added four tiger babies to the world's population."

Caught in his enthusiasm, Jade smiled. Their eyes met, the angry, hurting words dissolved. Then Jade remembered. Russ stepped back, turning away at the same time. Jade felt the rejection down to her toes.

"So what happens when you retire Monarch?" She rushed to speak, to blot out the pain.

Without looking at her, Russ shrugged. "Not much, really. He's not our only breadwinner, as you know. If this had occurred five years ago, we would be worried. As it is now, Hideaway has a solid reputation, and most of our stock are actively involved in promotion and film work. Besides, Sam and I occasionally get calls to train or retrain animals other than our own. That adds to the kitty."

By now they were almost to the barn. If she could just keep the subject going until Sam joined them. "I've heard about some rather unsavory practices to get animals to perform."

Russ gave her a sharp look. "There are always people around who don't play by the rules. For them, we have organizations to protect the animals. But remember, a maimed or disfigured animal is really a loss. His days of use are severely limited. Today's performing animals are athletes and actors schooled to do their jobs." He stopped in front of a large cage of sturdy bars with a wooden floor and vented, solid sides that lifted up. "As you can see from this—" he gestured toward the box "—every attempt is made to protect the animal in transit as well as provide for his comfort. These cages are sold by a company up north. They aren't made by us here at Hideaway." He moved away. "Are you ready to go to work now?"

Jade nodded while making a mental note to include a section in the article on training practices by others besides Russ. Fresh out of questions, she welcomed the physical activity. Russ took her at her word, passing her a bucket, brush and soap. For the next hour they worked side by side speaking only when necessary. Jade put all her energy into cleaning the shipping crate, but it wasn't enough to keep her from noticing the way Russ moved easily from one chore to the next. The sun was high in the sky, gilding his supple muscles and bringing a sheen of perspiration to his body. The hose they used to rinse had occasionally missed its target, and Russ's shirt was plastered to his chest, offering a visual temptation she wished she had enough willpower to ignore.

Russ was having problems of his own. His libido had discovered a definite craving for a slender woman in a wet shirt and equally drenched jeans. Jade hadn't worn a bra, a fact that had been too evident when the first spray had hit her. Try as he might he couldn't keep his eyes from the sway of her breasts as she scrubbed the cage. Every move she made reminded him of how she felt in his arms, the way she had clung to him, demanding all he had to give. Heat pooled between his legs, and no amount of intentional wetting with the cold water had cooled his hot blood one bit. Disgusted with his lack of control, he cleaned all the harder. It didn't help. How he was going to survive the time with her on this shoot was a question he didn't want to ask. Mentally damning the wanderlust that drove her, he turned the hose on full force to finish rinsing the cage.

Jade stepped out of the way. She had seen Russ's ferocious expression and wondered if it was as hard for him as it was for her. She hoped so. The idea that she was the only one suffering was unpalatable. She glanced at her hands. The slight tremor in her fingers told of her diminishing control. Despite everything, she wanted him now, here in the open where anyone could see.

"What next?" she blurted, needing a diversion before she disgraced herself.

Russ turned off the hose and began recoiling it. "Lunch, then Sam and I have a few chores around here to do. Nothing you could help with."

Jade took this refusal better than she had the other. "That will give me time to go into town and develop the film I shot this morning," she said, revealing none of her feelings. Without waiting for his acknowledgment, she started for the house. The memories just wouldn't leave her alone.

Lunch was as much an ordeal as Jade had expected. She escaped as soon as she could without arousing Emma's and Sam's suspicions. By keeping busy she was able to get through the rest of the day. The photographs of Monarch came out better than she deserved given her distraction. One, especially, caught her attention and brought the tears she didn't want to shed to her eyes. Russ stood framed against the sky, facing the tiger as it stood on its hind legs, towering above the man. If she'd had to title the photo, she would have called it "Danger Controlled." Monarch was primitive power held in check by the man he dwarfed. Russ looked up at the huge cat, his face calm, intent. He faced the danger, walked with it, courted it and then held it in his hands as surely as he had held her in his arms.

Jade stared at the photograph, letting the tears fall. Russ possessed the attributes of beauty, strength, gentleness and caring. It was more than she had ever thought to find in one person, and it was in this man. He had offered her a place with him. It didn't matter that he hadn't spoken of love or commitment. What mattered was that even now, she could not still the need to move on. She had held all that she valued in humankind in her hands, and she had tossed it back to the gods who had brought her and Russ together. Fool! The word filled her mind as the tears filled her eyes. In that moment she hated the gypsy she had become. For one impossible instant she almost believed she could ignore the voice that drove her on and take what was hers.

"I could do it," she whispered into the muted gloom of the darkroom. "I could make myself stay." She dropped the picture, knowing even as she said the words that they both deserved more than that. For a long moment she allowed herself the luxury of tears, then she raised her face and blinked back the moisture. Squaring her shoulders, she wiped her eyes with the back of her hands. She had made her choice. It would stand.

Jade finished the developing with plenty of the afternoon remaining. Although there wasn't much to see in the small town, she made herself stay. Every hour she was away from the ranch was one less block of time she had to endure seeing Russ. It was late, almost dinnertime when she returned to Hideaway. No one was in the hall when she arrived, so she made her way undetected to the guest room. A shower helped refresh her while the cream cotton dress with the tiered skirt inset with lace made her feel as cool as the weather wasn't. She entered the dining room just as Emma came out of the kitchen with the last platter of food. Feeling guilty for not being there to help, Jade apologized.

"No need," Emma denied with a smile. "I figured you were tied up with your pictures."

Sam came in, followed by Russ. "I wish I'd had a camera when these two were cleaning out Monarch's cage today," he remarked to his wife, holding a chair for her. "You would think they were playing in the water like two kids. They were drenched to the skin before they were done."

Jade sat before Russ could come around to her side of the table to duplicate Sam's actions. She had control now, but she'd lose it if he touched her.

"I always end up wet unless it's the dead of winter," Russ defended himself, trying not to notice that Jade was avoiding even the smallest, innocent touch. He should have been glad.

Sam chuckled. "Not that wet."

"Sam," Emma exclaimed, catching Jade's wince. "You shut up, you old fool."

"'Old fool,'" he repeated, grimacing. "Woman, I'll have you know that the only thing old about me is my age."

"And your brains," his wife replied, passing him the fried chicken.

Jade served herself, allowing the older couple to carry on their mock fight without her input. Russ seemed intent on the same course. Dinner passed slowly but, mercifully, Emma and Sam kept up their sparring. Jade excused herself early, on the grounds of needing to pack. Only then did she look at Russ. His eyes were dark, angry and as fed up with the situation as she. But he said nothing as she left the room. Jade paused in the hall to let out the breath she had hardly been aware of holding. Having seen the thought in his eyes, Jade had been afraid Russ would accompany her to her room.

"I have some paperwork I need to get done," Russ said to no one in particular as he got to his feet.

Sam glanced at him then at the door through which Jade had passed. "Sure, son," he replied with a knowing grin.

Russ responded in kind just to keep the pretense of peace with Jade alive before making his escape to his study. The room was a haven that even his friends did not invade. Russ poured himself a drink and sat behind the desk. By turning he could look out over his property, an occupation that was usually restful and very satisfying. But not tonight. He didn't want the land, peace or the life he had carved. He wanted the woman. Not just any woman but Jade, the gypsy, the wanderer, the restless wind.

Fool! How many times had he berated himself for what he had done. She had told him what she was that very first day. But had he listened? Not he! He had built a cage, thrust her in it, and been furious when she fought her way out. She was wild and free and had to stay that way to survive. Had he remembered that? Oh, no. Because he wanted her he had held her too tightly. And now she was gone but not gone. The pain of wanting her was like acid in his belly. Even now he was maneuvering her, trying to make her see what could be theirs. The anger of his own stupidity was corroding his thoughts and eating at his good sense.

An hour passed as he sat contemplating the situation. He heard Emma and Sam leave to go home to the small cottage a few hundred yards from the main house.

What was Jade thinking and feeling? He knew she hurt. Pain was in her every glance, in the shrinking from his touch, in the words she rushed to fill the silences with, in the way she stayed away rather than risk running into him. They could not go on this way. The pain rode both of them. Their desire was a fire that would not be quenched except in each other's arms. He had to face those facts, and so did she. He finished the last swallow of his drink and slammed the glass on the desk. Jade valued truth. He would make her listen to him and understand what they could still have for the time left to them. Stalking from the room, he traversed the hall and rapped once on her door before opening it.

Jade snatched the robe from the bed, pulling it around her nakedness as she whirled. "Russ, what are you doing?" she demanded angrily.

Russ crossed to her, not even noticing her unclothed state. He caught her arms and brought her against his chest. "You want me. I want you. What the devil are we doing to ourselves with this stupid denial business?"

Jade lifted her head, her eyes flashing storm warnings that only a fool would ignore. "How dare you stomp into my room and start on this again. I won't have it." She pushed at his arms, forgetting the robe she clutched. It slithered to the floor, unnoticed by either of them.

"Cut the outrage and answer me one question."

"Why should I?" She glared at him through a tangle of hair. She couldn't escape, but she was far from helpless.

"Because you're no coward," he returned bitingly.

"What's the question?"

"Do you want me?"

Jade opened her mouth to deny him, then stopped. She couldn't lie. "Yes, damn you, but I don't want to want you."

"That goes double for me, but what my head says and my body demands are two different things." He pulled her closer still, wrapping his arm around her waist as he crushed her breasts against his denim shirt.

Jade gasped at the contact of the rough fabric against her sensitive nipples. Desire flared. "Feel us. I hurt, Jade. You do, too. Let's put us both out of our misery."

"You're crazy."

"I am." His lips nipped at hers. "With wanting you. It hasn't been twenty-four hours and I hurt so badly I feel like I'm on a rack. Stop the torture, Jade. Come to me, if it's only for a few more days. I won't ask more than that."

"I'm not into pain, Russ. I hurt, too, and if we go back to what was, I'll hurt even more. I don't want that." She stayed motionless in his arms. They both knew he could make her weak with wanting, but knew, too, he wouldn't take that kind of advantage. Not now.

"We're not going back. Just forward. Eyes open."

She searched his expression. Could she do it? Could she accept his passion and forget that he wanted her to stay?

Russ waited, seeing the same questions he had confronted, seeing the same conclusions he had drawn. He inhaled slowly, letting the oxygen flow into his lungs as he allowed the desire to fill him. His hands moved over her back, stroking instead of imprisoning.

"Say it. I need to hear the words."

"I want you." Head up, Jade met the challenge. Lifting her arms, she slipped them around his shoulders. "I hurt, too." She gave him more than he asked because he did not demand this time. "Make the hurting stop."

Russ bent his head, taking the lips she offered. "Gladly, gypsy." With his endearment, Russ accepted that this time there would be no illusion of permanence to trick him into believing she would abide with him. This time he would take only what she would give, the passion he could make her feel, the desire she had for him. His hands molded her to him.

Jade softened, waiting for the tenderness, the loving to begin. What she found in his touch was wanting, a man's deep drive to possess a woman. Her body caught fire even as her mind screamed, "No, not like this."

Russ laid her down on the bed, taking her weight as he came down beside her. His hands tangled in her hair, holding her still as he drank the passion from her mouth. Her groan of need was a goad to take more. He couldn't get enough of her. His clothes were only a barrier for as long as it took him to strip them away. And then he was as naked as she. Her body glistened in the soft light of the bedside lamp as she twisted beneath him, arching with each stroke of his fingers across her sensitive skin. He smiled, enjoying the feel

of her as he thrust into her softness, for a moment
fusing them as one. Then he moved his hips, flexing
tautly until Jade cried out in pleasure.

"All of me, Jade. Take all of me," he said with a
sigh from above her.

Jade arched up, feeling him move deeper still. Her
arms were tight around his back, holding him to her
with every ounce of strength she possessed. "Love
me," she pleaded, wanting the tenderness as much as
the passion. The glitter in his eyes was exciting but
frightening, too. The passion that had consumed her
as much as it had warmed her in the past, now seared,
cutting deep in her soul until she could hold back
nothing from her lover. He possessed as surely as he
was possessed. And when they reached the summit of
desire there was no cry of her name upon his lips, only
a harsh groan of passion spent as she whispered his
name against his skin.

Jade lay there, feeling as though she had come
through a storm. The dreamy aftermath she had
known in the past with Russ was gone as if it had never
been. He lay beside her not moving, not touching, not
speaking. She lifted herself on her elbow, watching
him, wanting to ask what had happened but almost
afraid to hear his answer.

Russ rose silently and reached for the clothes that
lay strewn on the floor. He dressed without looking at
her. Jade stared at him, unable to believe he intended
to leave without a word to her. It was only when he
reached the door, she realized he really was going.

"Aren't you staying with me tonight?" she whispered, appalled to discover there were tears in her eyes.
She clutched the sheet to her breast, suddenly not
wanting him to see her nakedness.

Russ stopped, his back to her. "No. I figured you would want your privacy." He couldn't look at her and still leave. She wanted no ties, and he was doing his damnedest not to make any.

"But Russ..." Jade began helplessly, then paused, wondering what to say. "I don't mind, really." Mind! She wanted him to stay, to hold her, to sleep beside her.

He shook his head. "No. It's better this way, so I won't forget and ask more of you than you want to give."

Jade frowned and tried to get out of bed. She had a feeling if she could just touch him he would change his mind. The sheets tangled around her, trapping her. Frustrated, she yanked at the covers, for one moment taking her eyes from his back. By the time she was free he was gone, the door shut behind him. Jade gazed at it, feeling more pain than she had known existed. Wrapping her arms around her body, she tried to ward off the shivers that rippled over her skin. Tears welled in her eyes, but she didn't notice. All she could hear was the tiny click of the door when he had walked out.

Empty! More than a word it was a state of mind and body. Pain! More than a feeling, a way of breathing, of thinking. And why? Russ had given her what she asked for. In that moment she knew desire and passion were not enough. Not with Russ. She needed more. She needed the caring, the tenderness, the loving. But she had thrown those away, and now she was left with the ashes.

Dropping her head to a pillow still warm from his body, she cried as she never had in her life. Cried for what she had lost, for what she had become and for what she could not change. And when there were no more tears left she slept, alone and vulnerable. It was then the nightmare came. The hideous memory that haunted her, recalling destruction of beauty and life.

Jassimine, her friend. A woman with a child. A pretty little girl named Peace. A riverbank where the poor did their wash. The soldiers that shouldn't have been there. A journalist, American, playing with the child. A zealot who hated Americans because they were Americans. A rifle raised. Murder in the eyes of the youth who pointed it at the journalist. A shot. Peace destroyed by the bullet. Jassimine screaming, rushing to her child. Another shot. The journalist still lived. The woman who ran between Jade and the soldier died in the dust, her hand outstretched to the child she loved.

Run! Jade ran, her legs carrying her away before any more could go in her place. The bullets followed her, one nicking the building beside her, splintering a shard of concrete to pierce her foot. A scar to remind of Jassimine and her child. Memories. Hers. Guilt. Hers. Breathing hard, Jade awoke, the sobs choking her. Ahmand had hidden her as the soldiers had searched. He had buried his wife and child without a word, then bathed Jade's wound and nursed her through the fever that followed. She remembered it all as she stared around the bedroom, trembling and crying. The pain then had been as intense as the moment Russ had left her alone. She'd had no defense then and she had none now. She could only survive until tomorrow. Until she could do for Russ what she had not been able to do for Jassimine and Peace. She would search for and find the tenderness, the beauty,

the loving. Russ had felt it for her once, she would recall it for him now. For the time they had left she
would give him that even if it meant pain for herself
when their moments were done.

Nine

Jade's resolution was sorely tried the next morning. Russ made it clear from the moment he spoke to her at breakfast that while he was friendly, the intimacy they had shared no longer existed. Every attempt Jade made to soften him went unnoticed. Every special smile she sent his way was returned with one that acknowledged her without giving her any special importance. Russ spoke to her as he did to Sam and Emma. The caressing note in his voice that had been for her alone was gone—as were the little touches, the quick but explicit glances. By the time breakfast was over Jade was frustrated, torn over tackling Russ about his attitude and hurting because of the new role she had in his life. Jade frowned at the duffel bag she was packing, the one she should have packed the night before.

"What now?" She rolled the cotton shirt she held into a tight ball and stuffed it in the bottom of the bag. "I should be happy he's taking me at my word." Another garment met a similar fate. "But I hate it. I don't want to just be his sexual partner. Damn!" She rarely swore. "It's not supposed to be like this. It was supposed to be easier, less painful, not more so."

Finishing the chore, Jade fastened the bag, adding it to the pile by the door. All that she had brought with her was ready to go. She had learned long ago not to leave things in a place expecting to come back. Departures with little or no notice were an occupational hazard she had learned to live with. Clothes got expensive when she had to replace them because they weren't where she ended up.

"Jade, Russ is about ready to leave," Emma called, tapping lightly on the bedroom door.

"Coming." Jade slung her camera cases over her shoulder and lifted the duffel bag in the other hand. She had to go forward because she couldn't go back.

"Good grief, girl, are you trying to kill yourself?" Emma demanded, reaching for one of the cases.

Jade evaded her with a faint smile. "Believe it or not I'm used to heavier loads than this. I can manage." The smile took the sting from the refusal.

Emma frowned. "But you don't have to while you're with us. One of the men would have helped you if you had said something."

Jade ignored the offer, for there was no answer she could make without sounding rude and ungrateful. Emma lived in a household where the men recognized her contribution as a person and still helped out if she needed a hand. That wasn't Jade's world. She couldn't explain the difference so she didn't try.

Jade and Emma reached the yard in time to see Russ beginning to load Monarch. Fascinated despite her distraught state, Jade froze, watching the proceedings.

"He goes in so easily," she observed.

The big cage, large enough for the cat to move around in comfortably, was solidly attached to a specially built flatbed by steel cables. A semi bearing the ranch's logo would pull the rig the forty plus miles to Palm Beach International Airport where a DC-3 awaited them. From there it was more than three hours flying time to Atlanta.

Russ closed the cage door before turning to Jade. Despite being occupied with Monarch he had seen her arrive. For one second he had allowed himself to look his fill then he had turned his attention back to the tiger. He didn't want to remember the night before.

"He's used to it," he explained carefully.

He ignored the twist in his stomach at the sight of her bags stacked around her feet. It had taken only a glance to know that everything she had brought with her was packed and going to Atlanta with them. He wanted to know if she intended to leave for New York from there, but he forced himself not to ask. He had promised her that he wouldn't cage her, and he would keep his word even if every nerve was screaming in the agony of losing her. Suddenly realizing that both Emma and Jade were looking at him as though they expected him to say something more, he mentally groped for the subject that had brought him to Jade's side. Monarch's roar was a timely hint.

"For Monarch the cage represents safety. If he's threatened or his world is upset somehow, he'll return to it if he can. He's never known anything but warmth, food and approval in there," he added, turning to stare at the large box with its solid sides brought up to cover the bars. Roomy air vents allowed ventilation while the carrier was enclosed for shipping.

"You mean if you were hurt or he got loose, you could give him a command and he'd head for that?" Jade questioned, waving her hand in the direction of the trailer.

Nodding, Russ's lips twisted slightly. "He would if I could retain my authority enough in the first case to overcome his natural instincts."

Startled at the wording of his answer, she studied him. "What instincts?" She forced herself to ignore how tall and in control he looked. Her fingers clenched as she pushed away the memory of the feel of his skin beneath her hands.

Shrugging, Russ glanced at the cage and then back at Jade. "Wild creatures hunt, and even if they are bred in captivity they still have their instincts. But they also recognize power and respect it. I'm the king in Monarch's world only as long as I hold on to the right. A right I earned not by fear or pain," he clarified on seeing her perplexed expression. Although she had questioned him at length on his training techniques, they had never actually gotten to this. "He knows I respect him and what he can do. But occasionally he flexes his muscles. Most of the time nothing happens."

"But . . . ?" Jade prompted, not liking the feeling that was building in the pit of her stomach. "He has hurt you, hasn't he?" The telling silence went on so long that she hardly noticed that Emma suddenly found something pressing to do in the house.

"My God, that's how you know he'll go back to his cage. You sent him there." Horror flowed through her, as she remembered the long scar that began at the base of Russ's spine and curled around his left side to his hip. The soft chambray shirt and denims he wore obscured her sight, but nothing could erase the memory of the raking slash.

For just an instant he forgot his promise to her and himself. He saw only her pain and fear for him. He brought her hand to his lips, his eyes holding hers with unflinching directness as he placed a kiss in the center of her palm.

"Do you think your wounds are any less shocking to me?" he asked quietly as he folded her fingers over the gentle caress. "You've been in far more dangerous circumstances than I."

"But you don't have to do this. You have other animals," she countered, barely understanding her own words. She completely missed his references to her work. "You don't have to take these kinds of chances."

"Don't we?" One brow lifted while he watched her realize what she had said. "It hurts, doesn't it?" At her blank look he explained. "Knowing that someone you care about is deliberately courting trouble." He could no more have stopped his question than he could have held back the tides. "The difference between us is only that I can minimize most of my danger while you have no control over the risks in your environment."

Jade sighed deeply, unable to fathom the degree of worry flowing into every nerve and sinew. She had never really thought about her work or his in those terms. "We're fools, both of us," she said, frowning at the thoughts crowding her mind. Russ made her sound reckless, foolhardy. She didn't like the image.

Russ released her hand. He had to move away before he tried to forge another bond between them. She wanted only passion—not caring and understanding. He had to remember that. "Perhaps, but neither of us is going to change." He turned away. Keeping his promise should have been getting easier. Normally he was a patient man, but with Jade it seemed that he didn't have any patience at all. He wanted her so badly he could taste it. He hated backing off. He hated holding her in his arms and pretending that it was only her passion he wanted. He hated not feeling free to touch her, to kiss her just because she was near. But most of all he hated that she did not want more from him.

"Russ?" Jade saw the pain in his eyes just before he turned to stare at the tiger prowling the cage.

"Leave it, gypsy." He spoke without facing her.

She frowned, uneasy and tense. Nothing was going as she expected. "Why do you call me that?"

He looked at her then. "A reminder." Frustration and need mixed to add a sting to the answer.

It took a second for the words to make sense. Jade raised her hand to his cheek.

"No pity. You made the rules. I'm sticking to them."

Jade wanted to apologize and that confused her. What had she done wrong? "I've been honest with you." She groped to understand.

He inclined his head. "Oh, yes, you have been that," he agreed. "Your way or no way."

Jade drew back, angered at his comment. "I never said that," she tried to defend herself.

His sharp-eyed look dared her to hang on to the lie. "Didn't you?"

Jade inhaled at the mockery in his voice. "You don't have the right to do this to me."

"True. You won't allow me any rights at all. And fool that I am, I won't take what isn't mine to have." Without another word he walked away, leaving her standing in the driveway.

Jade stared after him, unable to think beyond the sound of his bitterness. Sam came up beside her, his eyes dark with sympathy. She started when he touched her arm.

"I've known Russ since he was a kid, and you won't find a finer man." He searched her face. "Maybe I should hold my peace, but I won't. Age must have some privileges." He waited. When Jade didn't draw away he continued. "I've watched you two these past weeks. For what it's worth, you belong together. Kinda like Monarch and Kismet. Don't know what the problem is. Emma and me ain't blind, you know, but if you care about him, don't rake him over the coals. A woman's got the power to really hurt a man who cares about her. And Russ, when he cares, cares deep. If you're worrying about him doing right by you, don't."

Jade wanted to say something, but the words just wouldn't come.

"He ain't had an easy life, you know. What you see here was built with sweat and blood and guts. He started out a teenager and ended up a man I would be proud to call 'son.'"

The words finally came, in a flood. "I don't know what you and Emma think is going on, but I can tell you that I know what Russ has done and I respect that. As far as our relationship is concerned, I respect that, too. But I can't pretend I'm going to be here forever just because he's a stayer and I'm a...a...gypsy." His word for her. The endearment that was a reminder. "I don't lie."

Sam watched her for a long minute, assessing her and the stand she had taken. Then he glanced in the direction Russ had gone, seeing him emerge from the barn. "You know, I like you, but right now I wish you hadn't come here. I really do." He touched his finger to the brim of his hat and then walked toward Russ without looking back.

Jade watched him go, not even hurt by his words. She understood and even admired the man who had the loyalty and courage to say what he thought. Sighing at what couldn't be changed, she bent and hefted her duffel.

"Let's get moving," Russ said, coming to take the bag from her. "We've got a plane to catch."

Jade didn't look at him as she handed over the satchel. Right now she wasn't even sure she wanted to look at herself. Sam pulled himself up to the driver's seat of the semi, not watching her, either. He had said his piece. Jade climbed in beside him, wishing things could have been different. She had enjoyed Hideaway and the people who created and cared for it. If she had been someone other than who she was she would have counted herself privileged to share a life with them. She glanced around the yard, saying goodbye. If the gods were merciful she would not be back, she would not see this place or feel its pull again.

Keeping her face free of her thoughts was a major effort. Jade hardly noticed that Russ had joined them in the cab. It was only when his leg pressed against hers that she realized that for the next forty miles she would be sandwiched next to him.

But he could have been on another planet for all the attention he paid her. He and Sam went over the last details about the ranch. Sam was to remain at Hideaway while Russ was in Atlanta. Jade listened for a while then gave up. It was safer to watch the scenery flash by. She didn't want to worry whether Sultana had a leg infection starting from the cut on the hind cannon. She didn't want to hear that the water level was getting low, that a drought might be in the future. She wanted freedom. She stared down the open road. She had always wanted freedom. She wanted to see the road stretching out before her.

She stopped, her mind focusing on the arrow-straight highway that split the Florida land. What was there out here? Beauty? Of a primitive kind, yes. But what else? She frowned, never having asked this question of herself before. What was it around the bend, over the horizon, beyond the sun? Were the cities really all that different? Were the wars really new, more in touch with the truth? Were the people in one country so very unique from those in another?

No!

One place, one person, a hundred of either. So much sameness. Motives, needs, climates, politics. The names differed but the things were the same. As she was. The same. Never changing. Never growing. Never sharing. Never touching any life but her own. She didn't have so much as an apartment. Just an address and that wasn't even her own. If she passed out of life today who would mourn her as Jassimine had been mourned? Only Irene and Daryl and her father. Not much for her years of existence.

She glanced at Russ and then at Sam. They would be mourned. They were loved and cared about. Could it be that the life she had seen as a cage was no cage at all? Could she have been so wrong all this time? Confused, uneasy and suddenly scared, she bit her lip. The cab was closing in around her, trapping her with her own thoughts. She couldn't escape. She could only think—too much, too long.

Jade hardly noticed the rest of the trip. It was only when Russ touched her knee, drawing her attention to the airport that lay spread before them that she realized they had reached their destination. Forcing her thoughts away, Jade obediently paid attention to the unloading process of the tiger. She still had a job to do despite the chaos of her life. She would do it. It seemed to be the only thing left that was stable enough to depend on.

Sam brought the rig to a stop at the rear of the DC-3 that would take them to Atlanta. The cargo door was open, revealing a large, empty cavern. As soon as the truck was parked, they got out, Sam to confer with the man who had directed them to the plane and she and Russ to check on Monarch.

"Joe suggests we take Monarch out and let them forklift the cage off the truck and as far up on the ramp as they can get it. Then they'll drag it in from there. Once it's strapped down, we can walk Monarch in."

Russ nodded after a moment's thought. "Sounds good."

Sam grunted his agreement. "Yeah, I don't think any of us want to go through that loading we had last month with Kismet. She damned near tore the cage apart when they tried to lift her and it at the same time.''

Jade closed her eyes briefly at the reminder she didn't want or need about the hazards of Russ's work. Stepping back out of the way while the men put their plan into action, she forced herself to take out her camera. Being careful not to disturb anyone, she aimed for the first shot of the operation. Despite her concentration, she couldn't help being impressed by the smooth transfer.

Monarch could have been a placid tabby cat for all the interest he showed in the mild flurry of activity going on around him. He stood statue-still at Russ's side, his coat a vivid splash of color in a world of metal birds and squat buildings. The disdain on his face and the regality of his posture made a beautiful shot. But once again Jade was struck by the comparison of the raw strength of the beast versus the intellect and authority of the man who commanded him. ''Nature's Creation Harnessed but Not Tamed by Man.'' The title sang in her mind as the shutter clicked. A moment later, Monarch's cage was set in place and strapped down to await its occupant. With a quiet command, Russ led the big cat docilely up the ramp as the ground crew watched in awed silence. Smiling to herself, Jade followed them into the belly of the plane. She knew how they felt. She had been, and still was, amazed at Russ's ability to handle the tiger. Whatever the future held she knew she would always remember Russ's skill.

''I guess you've been right all along,'' she conceded as she sat down next to him.

Surprised, Russ glanced at her. Had she finally understood him? Was that why she had been so preoccupied on the trip to the coast? One look at her face was enough to tell him her comment had nothing to do with what he was thinking. Disappointed, determined not to show it, he asked, "How?"

Jade fastened her seat belt before answering. "About Monarch. He's been as well behaved as you said he would be."

Both of them looked toward the cage where the tiger lay in uncaring leisure. Showing neither concern nor interest, he simply stared back at them.

"I think he likes to travel." Russ shrugged, dismissing the subject. He didn't want to talk about the cat. He wanted to talk about them. Damn his promise. She was so close. He could have her in his lap where she belonged. He stared out the window, wishing he was holding her, wishing she were a million miles away so he wouldn't be thinking of her.

Jade sighed when he turned away. For a moment she had seen a glimpse of the Russ she wanted to be with. Not this new, friendly, but uninvolved man who sat beside her. "Russ, can't we—" she began, ignoring the lift of the plane as it left the ground.

Russ swung his head around. "Can't we what, Jade?"

She couldn't put it into words. "You know."

He shook his head, almost glad to see her stumble for a reply. Her self-possession was beginning to wear thin. He wanted her rattled by him. "What's wrong?"

She spread her hands, needing his help and suddenly realizing she didn't even know how to ask for it. "You're treating me like you don't want to be around me anymore." She had said it. Would he understand?

"It's like you said. I want you but I don't want to want you."

Her eyes filled before she even realized she was hurt. His expression changed so subtly that if she had not been watching him closely she would have missed it. Hope trickled in to dilute the pain. Maybe she deserved his revenge.

"Why are you crying? I'm giving you what you said you wanted."

Jade blinked. "I never said I wanted..." She stopped, unable to describe his attitude in words that would make sense to either of them. "You left me last night. You talk to me as if I were Emma or Sam."

Russ sighed, seeing she really didn't understand him at all. She truly was hurt by the very thing she professed to want. That knowledge more than any other gave him some comfort. "How do you want me to treat you? If I act the lover I put ties on you that you tell me you don't want. If I take you to bed without anything but passion between us you see me as unfeeling. If I don't touch you at all it's rejection. How do I win? How do I meet your rules?"

Self-knowledge is never easy, and in Jade's case it came like a strike of flint against a rock. She suddenly realized how selfish she had been. She had been alone so long, dependent on no one, that she had forgotten what it was like to care about someone else. In all her calculations she hadn't considered what she was asking of Russ.

"I'm so sorry," she whispered, aching to touch but afraid to.

"I know." Russ sighed. Her tears were more disarming than her apology. But he couldn't afford to be swayed.

"Sam was right. I never should have come."

"No. I'm glad. I think you'll do more for the article than anyone else Worth could have sent."

"Is that the only reason?" The question escaped before Jade could stop it. She didn't want to examine why she had to know.

"What other reason do you want?"

Stalemate.

Jade almost backed off but at the last second changed her mind. She couldn't take anymore of the emotional roller coaster they were on. "I don't want what happened last night to happen tonight," she said honestly.

"Neither do I," he returned swiftly, glad to bring the situation out into the open. "I don't like feeling like a stud." The words were harsh but accurate.

"I never asked you to leave like that," Jade snapped, angered at the description. "I wanted you to stay."

"You don't know what you want. If I had stayed, I would have been acting just as I did over the weekend. You threw that back in my face, remember?"

Jade did, too well. "It didn't need to be as cold-blooded as last night," she returned, driven to defending herself.

"Tell me how, Jade." He turned, catching her arms so that she could not escape. "We tried it your way and mine. Neither of us liked the other. Tell me what we can try now."

She had no answer. The pain of his grip was small compared to the hurt in her heart. She hadn't wanted to care about this man or any man, but she did. Too much. She couldn't tell him, but she could finally admit her feelings to herself. She'd been a fool to think it only passion and desire that made her tremble in his arms. Desire would not have given birth to the tears she had shed over him. Wanting would not have taught her the meaning of the loneliness when loving became an act of mating. Warmth would not have turned into the coldness of an empty bed when he left her once they had drunk their fill of passion.

"Then what do we do? Forget we ever came together?"

"Yes."

"Can you do that?" she whispered, wondering if she had the strength to forget the way he felt when he took her in his arms. Could she forget the desire that had rocketed her to a place she had never traveled? Could she forget the caring and the tenderness he had shown her? Could she forget the way he had held her when the nightmare of Jassimine had haunted her until she cried out?

"What other choice is there?" Even now he hoped she would give him the smallest inch. One hint of uncertainty and he'd make her acknowledge what existed between them. But there was no hesitation in the eyes she turned to his. Only pain and a fatalistic acceptance that told him too much. He released her as suddenly as he had taken her.

Jade fell back against the seat, her breath whooshing out in a long gasp.

"I'm going to take a nap. I didn't sleep well last night." Russ tossed the remark over his shoulder as he curled against the window and closed his eyes. When he woke up he'd face the woman who hadn't cared enough to let him into her life. He'd smile and be the man she had come to interview. He'd remember his work and all the reasons why Hideaway had to succeed.

He would not remember the silken feel of her body beneath his or the words she never spoke even in the grip of passion that made her body tremble like a leaf in the wind. He would remember only her skill with a camera and the images she drew with her pen.

Ten

Jade entered the trailer that she and Russ had been assigned for the shoot. Since Sam usually accompanied Russ on these trips, the production company had arranged for them to bunk together, as usual. Whether Russ had simply forgotten about the routine or had chosen to ignore the situation, Jade wasn't sure and she couldn't ask. Russ was seeing to Monarch's needs, leaving her to catch the first glimpse of their sleeping quarters. She stared at the compact space wondering how they were going to manage. There were twin beds at the rear, a bath off the small hall, a tiny kitchen and a postage-stamp-size lift-up table in front of the couch. Three days ago she would have enjoyed the enforced intimacy of the accommodations. Now she was seriously considering the merits of pitching a tent. Only the thought of what she would be betraying kept her from turning the idea into reality.

Sighing, she headed down the hall to place her duffel bag on one of the beds. Maybe she should be counting her blessings that the arrangements hadn't been even more intimate. There could have been only one bed. She smiled grimly, knowing it wouldn't have made much difference for all the interest Russ was showing in her.

He wasn't ignoring her. He quite simply, through some magic formula of his own, was acting as though she were a valued friend. He had introduced her to the crew when they had arrived and made sure she had a direction before taking off after Monarch. He had smiled, joked and, at one point, thrown an arm around her shoulders when one of the men had complimented her. But there had been nothing in his gesture that the most prim woman alive could have found exciting. Jade frowned as she carefully stored her cameras in the closet. Her clothes could stay in the bag since all of them were uncrushable. She had just finished the last of her unpacking when Russ came into the trailer without knocking. She glanced up, startled. He raised a brow but made no comment.

"Unless you're real big on cooking, we can eat at the commissary tent," he said when he joined her in the bedroom. He slung his one case on the other bed, unzipped it and pulled out a change of clothes. "Do you want the shower first or shall I?"

"You take it." If he could be casual so could she. She turned away as he started to unbutton his shirt. "And as far as the cooking goes, it doesn't matter to me where we eat just as long as we do."

Russ inclined his head, even managing a smile although it didn't reach his eyes. "My sentiments exactly." He tossed his shirt on the floor before kicking off his shoes. "Leave these things here. I'll get them when I come out. Monarch made a bit of a mess, so I don't want to put them in with the rest of our clothes." Jade glanced first at him and then at the garments on the floor, just as he knew she would. The flare of desire in her eyes when she saw his bare torso was a bittersweet triumph.

Jade looked away, wishing she hadn't allowed her curiosity to overcome her good sense. "I think I'll wait until after dinner to shower."

Russ shrugged. "Suit yourself." Whistling softly, he entered the minuscule room and closed the door.

Jade stood staring at it in silence. Three days and two nights. She'd never make it.

The first night was every bit as hard as she had feared. Dinner was no problem. There were too many people around for either her or Russ to be uncomfortable. He showed no sign of awkwardness, so apparently, she was the only one affected. Russ laughed and joked, clearly enjoying the company. Waiting until he was occupied with a group of men over coffee, Jade excused herself to return to the trailer. She had decided that if she could get in and out of the shower and into bed before Russ arrived, she just might be able to keep to the plan he had laid out for them. She made it, just. He entered as she was slipping under the covers. He paused in the doorway, staring at her.

"You realize that it's only nine o'clock."

There was enough mockery in his voice to make Jade wish she dared return the favor. Only the thought of what she might stir up kept her silent. She inclined her head, wishing she had looked at the clock. In truth, she had felt it to be late. The hours had certainly seemed to drag by. "I'm tired. I didn't nap on the plane like you did," she defended herself. A lame excuse was better than none at all.

Russ knew she was lying and almost tempted to call her on it. If he had thought it would do any good, he would have.

"I could use an early night, too, I guess." He started unbuttoning his shirt.

Jade watched him because she couldn't help herself. He was as beautiful to her as the tigers he worked with. He was also dangerous to her emotional health. She shut her eyes, only to open them again at the sibilant sound of a zipper being lowered. His jeans followed the course of his shirt. "What are you doing?" she croaked.

He glanced over his shoulder at her. "Undressing, of course. You didn't expect me to sleep in my clothes, did you?"

"No, but I didn't expect a private strip show, either," she snapped, physical frustration getting the better of her temper.

He grinned. "Then don't look."

Jade opened her mouth then shut it again. Giving a long-suffering sigh, she rolled onto her side and pulled the covers over her head. His laugh only added to her irritation. The rustle of clothes seemed unnaturally loud in the close confines. Jade breathed deeply, carefully, wishing she had the kind of experience to carry this scene off. She wished, too, that she could affect Russ the way he did her with the simplest of acts. The click of the light switch barely impinged on her consciousness. But she did hear the mattress beside her bed depress and the sheets whisper over a bare male form. How did she know he was nude? The images danced in her mind. She knew too well he detested the restrictions of pajamas.

"You can uncover your head before you suffocate," Russ said, turning on his side to watch her huddled form. He grinned in the darkness as she slowly pulled down the sheet.

"You did that on purpose," she accused. It was dark in the trailer, but she could hear the tone of his voice and see the flash of white that signaled a smile at her expense.

Russ studied her. "And if I did?"

She never should have said a word, Jade decided. He had been waiting for her to make a comment. "Nothing," she muttered, closing her eyes with more determination than desire. "Five-thirty comes early. I, for one, could use some sleep."

"Coward." His voice was soft, an invisible caress to reach out and enfold Jade.

Jade ignored the temptation even if she couldn't ignore him. Five-thirty was beginning to look like years away. When his steady breathing told her Russ had trotted off to dreamland without a thought she felt like slinging a pillow at him. Rat! Why did she have to be the only one lying awake wishing that their twin beds had suddenly been transformed into a double? Turning on her side so her back was to him, Jade punched her pillow. The bed was lumpy, the night too silent. And she was lonely. He could have at least said goodnight. She made another poke at her pillow and sighed. The mattress was a backbreaker. She frowned and considered the merits of the couch. Rolling over, she eyed the dark hall. Russ would never know—or care—where she slept.

Deciding anything was better than where she was, Jade eased carefully out of bed and padded, sheet and all, to the sofa, which stretched the width of the front of the trailer. A few minutes later, she knew that neither palate was at fault. She should have insisted on separate accommodations when she had realized that there was only this trailer allotted to them. She could have spent the night in a hotel. Groaning tiredly, she got up, picked up the sheet and trailed back to her bed.

"Can't sleep?"

She started at the quiet question. "I thought you were asleep." She glared at him wondering how long he had been awake. Barely able to make out his face, she tried to focus on the voice. Was that laughter she heard?

"I was, but all your moving around is too noisy." He raised himself on one elbow. "Something wrong with your bed?" he asked innocently. If her problem was anything like his own the best mattress in the world wouldn't have cured it. Frustration and desire were the ingredients for acute insomnia.

Jade threw the sheet over the bunk and started to get in. "It's like a rock, if you must know."

Smiling to himself, Russ reached out and slipped an arm around her waist before she could protest. Jade gasped as he hauled her down beside him. "Then, in the interests of my rest and yours, sleep here. This one is feather soft." A small lie but she wouldn't know. And once she was in his arms where she belonged, he knew she wouldn't care about the truth.

Jade pushed against his shoulders before she could lose her will to escape. The heat of his body wrapping around her was a potent seduction. She could already feel herself softening against him. "You're out of your mind. We've been all through this."

He ignored her, tucking her struggling length firmly against his and trapping her legs with a thigh thrown over them. "Shut up, woman, and quit squirming before you get us both into trouble."

Jade froze. There was no doubt about the kind of trouble he had in mind. "I can't sleep like this," she hissed. Sleep was the last thing on her mind.

"Well, I can." He settled himself beside her. "Stay awake if you want, but lie still."

Jade didn't think he meant it. But the gentle whisper of his breath against her neck a few moments later was irrefutable proof. The man was asleep. She was trying not to cuddle against him, and he didn't even notice. Irritated at him for not caring and at herself for wanting him to care, Jade glared into the darkness. But it was impossible to resist the peace that was stealing over her, the need to sleep that was suddenly weighing her lashes. The glower became a tiny smile as her eyes closed and she gave in. Her last coherent thought was that she really did need her sleep. Tomorrow promised to be a very interesting day. Besides, he was right about his bunk. It was nicer than hers.

Jade awoke slowly, aware of a deep feeling of contentment. The bed beneath her was soft and warm. She reached out a hand, knowing the reason she had slept so well. Russ. Her fingers groped, encountering only empty space. Her eyes popped open.

"Breakfast in ten minutes," Russ announced, watching her from the door. "You'd better get a move on or you'll miss the first call."

He turned away before she could say anything, a bittersweet smile on his lips. He had seen her look and the hand she had reached out to him when she was half asleep. Whether she knew it or not, Jade was more involved with him now than when she had really shared his bed. Then, she had reached for him in passion. But this time, he suspected, there had been more in her touch. For the first time since he had made himself get out of bed this morning, he was glad he had left her. If he had been there they would have just made love again, repeated the expressions of desire that had entangled them so well and so futilely in the past.

Jade watched him leave, beginning to hate his ability to walk away from her. Irritation returned as she got up and dressed. The day that had promised to be so intriguing was not starting out well at all. The commissary was noisy. There was no time to see Russ, much less talk to him. And the guide their director had sent her was more interested in the various gorgeous men on the shoot than she was in explaining to Jade what was going on. By the time the woman had shown her the vantage point from which she could watch the proceedings, Jade was holding on to her temper with both hands. And that wasn't like her at all. It didn't help to see her guide report to Russ that she was in place.

Jade sat on the small camp chair watching the miniature army of people prepare the scene for the commercial, forcing herself to concentrate on the action going on around her. The sooner she blocked Russ out of her mind the quicker she would settle down. She focused on Conner, the poster-perfect male, chosen as the image of the new cologne, El Tigre. He had just stepped out of the makeup van with his female partner for the shoot, a sultry-eyed model with long legs and an untamed look in keeping with her scanty primitive costume. Russ and Monarch were the only pool of silence in the area as they stood off to one side. Technicians aligned lights to eliminate shadows in some places and create others where needed. The director and his assistant were conferring, frequently making sweeping and often dramatic gestures, in the middle of a beehive of activity. The duo halted momentarily as the two human stars joined them. A moment later, the director crossed to within speaking distance of Russ, his wary eyes on the motionless tiger.

He swallowed, backed up a step and then explained exactly what the scene would entail. "Con will come through those trees with Monarch at his side. He stops when he sees Sandra in the clearing. Monarch growls, Con quiets him with a word, I hope, before he commands him to sit. Con walks slowly toward Sandra, the camera zooms in for tight shot as her wildness changes to docility. Con kisses her passionately, etc., etc., then he takes her back through the trees in his arms with Monarch tamely following them. Any questions?" He scanned the people in front of him, waiting.

Russ stifled a sigh. It hadn't taken him two minutes after being introduced to the director to decide he hoped he didn't have to work with the man too often. What he knew about animals would probably fit on the head of a pin with room left over for the Constitution.

"No, it's clear enough. I've already briefed Con on what to do, and since this is a voice-over commercial my giving commands off camera will be even less of a problem for the editing staff than usual," Russ pointed out calmly, more to soothe the nervous man before him than to impart knowledge of which each was fully aware.

The director was clearly still leery of the big cat. "You're sure he's tame?"

Shrugging, Russ evaded the question. "He won't cause any problems," Russ promised while wishing the director wasn't so new at working with exotic animals. Con and his wife, Sandra, and a few of the crew had been on several shoots with them over the past two years and were accustomed to Monarch. It made his job a lot easier if everyone knew what to expect.

"Then let's get to it," the director announced, stepping back a few paces before he was brave enough to turn his back on the jungle predator.

One brow arched sardonically, Russ watched the man hurry away. Glancing at Jade, he caught her watching him. The sun glinted off her hair, gilding her skin with gold. She looked untouched by the turmoil around her, in control, with that look of attention that was uniquely her own. There was little of the woman who had slept so sweetly in his arms the night before. For one second he allowed himself to mourn the loss and then with a shrug he tucked her away in his mind. He had work to do. He couldn't stand around staring at the woman he wanted so badly he could taste it. Commanding Monarch to walk, Russ headed for the small circle of trees where Conner awaited him.

"Hi ya, big guy," Con greeted the jungle beast like a pet kitty, although he didn't make the mistake of treating the tiger like one. Standing completely still, Con allowed Monarch to catch his scent through the formal tuxedo he wore. When Monarch gave a decided sniff of acceptance, he relaxed with a rueful grin. "I always wonder if he's going to bite me or lick me," he confessed honestly.

Appreciating how he felt, Russ grinned. He liked Con, and before the model had married Sandra they had shared some bachelor evenings when they were on a shoot together. "I feed him before we work, just so you'll remain intact. I wouldn't want Sandra to take a piece of my hide if I let anything happen to you with one of my animals."

Conner chuckled, glancing across the clearing to his scantily clad wife. His eyes kindled with memories that were too clear.

The love in the other man's expression cut Russ like a knife. He wanted Jade the way Conner wanted Sandra. But for them there would be no happy ending, no happily ever after. Russ leaned down to unbuckle the heavy collar around the tiger's neck and draped it and the chain around his own shoulders. He had to stop thinking about Jade. There was no future in it.

"Quit gawking at your wife," Russ ordered, straightening.

Con's smile broadened. "I'm not gawking. I'm drooling," he corrected unrepentantly.

Russ glared at him before he shook his head. "You two are indecent."

"If I hadn't seen Jade I'd think you were jealous, buddy."

Russ opened his mouth to reply but the director got in first, calling for quiet on the set.

"Time to earn my keep," Con whispered cheerfully, taking his place.

With a command to Monarch to stand, Russ moved out of camera range. From his position he could walk parallel with Con while working his charge. On the call for action, they began their stroll. All went well until the point where Monarch was supposed to growl. He didn't. Instead he sat down with a wide yawn. Russ called Monarch's attention back to him and they tried the scene again.

Jade followed the proceedings with interest, having never seen a commercial in the making before. The patience and professionalism shown by Conner and Sandra as Monarch muffed another take was impressive. Not so with the director. He had a scowl on his face at the end of the fourth attempt that mirrored his obvious frustration. The crew broke for a hurried lunch then everyone was back in place ready to begin again. The short rest made no noticeable improvement in Monarch's timing. It was late, and when the eighth and final try succeeded, every member of the staff breathed a weary sigh of relief.

Russ, with Monarch collared on his chain leash at his side, came down the path as the technicians were beginning to gather up their equipment. Russ stepped into the clearing just when someone bumped into one of the lights, knocking it over and causing the bulb to shatter on impact. The resulting explosion set off a chain of events that slowed time to an agonizing pace as the waning afternoon became a nightmare of confusion. A woman screamed. The twin, earsplitting noises coming on top of each other startled Monarch. He reared back trying to escape. When Russ dug in his heels and threw his strength against the lead, the cat was caught off balance. One front paw flashed out and caught Russ, slashing through his denims to the fleshy part of his upper thigh. Everyone froze in horror, Jade included.

The river of crimson darkening the blue fabric jerked her into action. Covering the space between herself and Russ in three strides, she skidded to a halt a few feet from the struggling pair. Talking quietly, she sought to blend her voice with Russ's as he fought to calm the panicked cat. Forcing her feet to cross the last few steps slowly when all she wanted to do was race to Russ's aid, Jade got a hold on the tail of the chain to lend her weight and balance to Russ's efforts. A white-hot pain shot through her shoulders from the pull of the five-hundred-pound Bengal on the other end. Gritting her teeth, she hung on, tugging backward toward the cage so close and yet so far away. Inch by inch, she and Russ gained ground as Russ's calming litany began to reach through the feline frenzy. Then it was over as Monarch spotted his home at the same time Russ commanded him in. With a lithe bound the tiger was through the open door and to the far side of the cage, his sides heaving with the remnants of fright and exertion. Russ slammed the panel shut and locked it.

He whirled around and caught Jade's shoulders, shaking her once, hard. "You crazy woman! You could have been killed!"

Jade barely heard him, her eyes were on his leg and the mark of the tiger on his skin. She pulled out of his arms, going on her knees before him. "I don't think he got you very deep, thank God," she muttered, ripping his pant leg open to the seams. Where she got the strength she didn't know or care. All she knew was that Russ was bleeding and it could have been so much worse. Her stomach roiled but she hardly noticed. Russ was all that mattered.

Eleven

————

Conner was the first one to reach them. "This should help." He thrust a white towel into Jade's hands before lifting Russ's arm over his shoulder and taking half his weight.

"I'm all right," Russ protested, still feeling the effects of knowing Jade had risked her life to save his. The scratch on his thigh was nothing compared to what might have happened to her.

Jade efficiently folded the pad and pressed it to the long, angry-looking wound. "I need something to tie it with," she said tersely, without glancing up.

"This do?" Once more Conner came to her rescue by stripping off his tie.

Jade took it with a muttered thanks. The makeshift bandage held. Pleased but worried, she rose and looked over Russ's face. Expecting to see a grimace of pain, maybe even a little paleness, she was startled at the anger still blazing out of his eyes.

"Russ?" she questioned in a strained tone. She moved to his other side without taking her gaze from his.

"Save it, Jade," Russ bit out between clenched teeth, his features tight with pain and anger.

Sucking in her breath at the harsh command, Jade said nothing more as they made their way awkwardly to the trailer and up the steps. Con took the brunt of Russ's weight when they lowered him onto the sofa.

"I'll get someone to bring a car over to the door in case he has to go to the hospital for stitches," Con offered quietly. "You look like you can handle Russ better than the rest of us."

There was curiosity in his voice but Jade didn't notice. She only nodded without looking away from Russ's face. "I'm going to clean away the blood so we can see what kind of damage Monarch did," she said, studying him worriedly. She didn't see Con leaving. "Okay?"

Russ met her eyes, unable to let go of the fear that had filled him when he realized who had come to his aid. "Why did you do it?"

"There was no other choice," she answered with brief simplicity. "You were in trouble." Touching his arm lightly, she felt the sting of tears. "I care about you," she whispered as though it were a secret. "I didn't want you hurt." The words were ones she had never spoken to any man. Panicked without understanding why, she got to her feet when Russ reached out for her. She couldn't let him touch her. Not now.

Finding the first aid kit took a minute and gave her an opportunity to pull herself together. Russ needed her.

Russ saw the trapped expression in her eyes and grimaced with pain that had nothing to do with his wound. He had gotten more from her with just those few words than all the moments they had shared in passion. Would she ever stop running? Would she ever see him and what he offered her as more than a cage to imprison her?

"Sometimes, I don't understand you," he said hoarsely. He stared at her, willing her to look at him. When she finally did, there was nothing in her eyes he could hold on to. She had escaped him again in a way he couldn't stop.

"I don't understand myself." Jade bent her head, not wanting to see what her admission would bring. Instead she concentrated on the things she could give him. Comfort and gentleness, perhaps even healing.

There was no answer, no reply to her truth. Sitting still Russ watched her work over him, hardly feeling the sting of the gauze moving over his torn flesh. Would this need to reach out to her ever leave him in peace? Would he ever give up on her? The answer was no. Until the moment she got on that plane to take herself away from him he still had a chance. He meant to make use of every second.

"It's going to need sewing up." Jade spoke quietly, almost normally. If there was a deeper note in her voice she hoped only she heard it. She rose, taking her supplies with her.

Russ nodded, giving one cursory glance to the wound. "I know. Let Con drive me into town. You've done enough for one day." And I can't take anymore right now, he added silently. I need to think, to plan.

Jade turned. "That's the last time you're going to shut me out," she said, suddenly angry. "I'm going with you."

"Why?" He watched her intently. Her reaction was unexpected but not unwelcome. Another sign of hope, another wall coming down. One day there would be no more.

Jade frowned, not understanding. "What do you mean, why? You'd go with me. I'm the only one here." She shook her head. "Who else would go with you?"

"Con."

"He won't be able to stay with you. He's got Sandra."

He opened his mouth then shut it again as the throbbing in his leg became a shaft of pain. "All right, you can come. But I don't need anyone to stay with me. Especially you." His eyes were closed or he would have seen the expression of hurt that flashed across Jade's face.

Jade went to the door to call Con, more confused than ever. Just when she thought she had found the answers to herself and Russ, he threw her another curve. Or she threw herself one, she added as she sat beside Russ in the back seat while Conner drove them into Atlanta. The realization of how much she wanted to be there for Russ was astounding. She couldn't remember the last time she had had a need to care for someone. Yet from the moment she had seen Monarch claw Russ she hadn't given her freedom a thought. All she had wanted was to help, to be at his side, to heal him. Those were commitments. Traps. Dependency on someone for more than just passion. Ties. She glanced sideways at Russ's face. The pain etched it with harsh lines. She wanted to soothe away his distress. Her arms ached to hold him.

"We're here," Con announced, pulling into the parking area of the emergency entrance. Moving swiftly he got out and came around to help Russ out of the car. Jade went ahead to alert the staff.

In moments Russ was whisked away while Jade struggled to fill out the forms necessary to admit him. Finally, she and Con were sitting in the waiting room. Or, at least, Con was sitting. Jade paced, relentlessly.

"Let me get you some coffee," Con offered.

Jade shook her head. "What's taking them so long?" She turned to glare at the wide set of doors that separated her from Russ. She'd never been good at waiting.

Con rose, going to take her hands in his. "You're shaking," he murmured in surprise. She had been so calm, so efficient when the accident happened, reacting before any of them had moved. "He'll be all right, I promise you."

Jade inclined her head, more in reflex than belief. "I know."

Studying her silently for a moment, Con came to a decision. "You love him, don't you."

Jade stared at him in shock. "No!" She snatched her hands from him, backing away. "You're way off the beam. We're just friends."

"If you believe that then I have a bridge that I could sell you in Brooklyn." He watched her closely, wondering why she would deny something so obvious.

"I've seen the way you look at each other. Hell, if I had been on the end of that chain today and Sandra had been in your place, I'm not sure she would have risked her life the way you did, and I know she loves me."

"I'm used to risks. That didn't mean a thing."

"My God, you really believe that, don't you?" he exclaimed in amazement.

"I know it. Russ explained how we met to you, about my work and the article. How could I be anything else in his life?"

"If I've learned one thing it's that we can do or be anything we want in the world. As long as we want it enough to fight for it, to give not take and to think with our hearts as well as our heads." Conner studied her, pitying her for her cynicism. "No one reaches our age without collecting a few bumps along the way, learning things we'd rather not know. It makes us cautious, and, sometimes, afraid. It doesn't have to make us blind."

"Sounds good on paper, but humans aren't paper dolls. Just wanting something is never enough. Common ground is important. A willingness to compromise. I've forgotten how if I ever knew it." She sighed, turning away. "I'll be leaving soon. Russ won't. It's that simple."

Con grabbed her shoulder and turned her to face him. "What do you mean, leaving?" he demanded.

"I phoned Emma and Sam to tell them about the accident. There was a call from my agent. There's a problem in Central America. I may have to go down there in the next few hours."

"You'd leave him now? Isn't there someone else who could go?" Jade was outside his experience. He couldn't believe she would really desert Russ when he was hurt.

"I'd leave him now. It's my job. I have to go." Jade said the words that should have been easy as though they were acid on her tongue.

Con dropped his hand, his expression almost condemning. "Was I ever wrong about you. I thought Russ had finally struck gold. Just shows how wrong a guy can be." He moved away to take a seat two down from the one he'd had.

Jade stood there and took his comments without defending herself. She deserved them, and in a way she was glad Con had said what he did. He cared about Russ and thought she was hurting him.

"Will you take care of him?" she asked quietly, knowing the answer but needing to be sure.

He glanced at her, not prepared to be kind. "Will it matter to you if I say no?"

"Yes." She looked at him, hiding nothing.

Con sighed, raking his fingers through his hair. He didn't understand this woman who faced him without apology. "I can't figure you out."

If Jade had been in a smiling mood she would have smiled at the words she had heard on Russ's lips and in her own mind too often.

"Yes, both Sandra and I will stay with him if it's necessary."

Jade nodded before resuming her pacing. In that second she knew the truth. Con had stumbled on what she had been trying to hide from herself. She loved Russ. Stupidly, foolishly and futilely. She wasn't good for him. If she told him how she felt he would do everything in his power to get her to stay with him, and feeling the way she did she would surrender to the magic he could weave. But one day, it wouldn't be enough. The restlessness would ride her again and she'd be away leaving him behind. She couldn't take the risk. She wasn't that brave. She couldn't love him knowing one day she would hurt him more than he deserved and more than she could live with.

"Ms. Hendricks?"

Startled at the intrusion, Jade turned to the doorway to find the doctor staring at her questioningly.

Jade searched his weary features. "Is he all right?"

He smiled faintly, a kind of exasperated humor chasing the exhaustion from his face. "He has quite a few stitches in his tough hide, a lacerated temper and a couple of puncture wounds from two shots he didn't want. He won't stay overnight, although I assured him it was only a precaution. He said you would take care of him." He peered at her from beneath silvered brows. "I can see that he's right." Shrugging, he conveyed his acceptance of the situation, though nothing could erase his professional disapproval.

"Are there any special instructions?" Jade asked, not wanting to put her agreement into words. If she did have to leave, Russ would be in hands as good if not better than her own.

"The nurse will give you a sheet. He's had an injection for pain, so he'll be drowsy for a while. Sleep's the best thing for him, besides staying off that leg as much as possible. He tells me the two of you and the tiger will be leaving for Florida late tomorrow."

Jade's mind went blank. In all her calculations she had forgotten Monarch. Unless she called Sam to fly to Atlanta there was no one else but her to help Russ get the tiger back home. A few weeks ago, even a day ago, she might have had an easy decision. She would have called Sam. Tonight, her love for this man clear in her mind, she knew what she had to do.

"I'll handle it, Doctor," Jade said firmly. "He won't do anything he shouldn't." She ignored Con's look of shock and the slow, growing smile that followed it. "Is he ready to leave now?"

The man nodded. "I can see he's in good hands."

"Loving hands," Conner muttered just loud enough for Jade to hear.

A few moments later, a nurse wheeled Russ out in a wheelchair. Jade studied his drawn features and knew the doctor hadn't understated the case at all. Russ looked like a battle-scarred warrior as he sat enthroned in the chair the hospital insisted on and he objected to. One jeans' leg was chopped off just barely past the point of decency to reveal the broad bandage on his thigh. He was rumpled with a drug-induced sleepy look that took years from his age and had Jade wishing she could take him in her arms and comfort him. His bitten-back groan when he finally settled himself in the back of the car, his head upon her breast and his leg stretched out across the seat, made her hurt with him. Unconsciously, Jade gathered him closer, taking pleasure in his sigh of relaxation as he went limp against her. For right now she could give him all the love she had in her heart without worrying that she would betray herself.

"Are you all right?" she asked huskily.

"I am now," Russ replied, his words slurring slightly under the influence of his medication.

Beyond their small exchange, no one spoke while Con headed back for the site. Jade was glad of the silence and the weight of the man she held. She had been so afraid when she had seen Monarch swipe at him. For the first time in her life she had actually been paralyzed in her terror for someone. The knowledge of how vulnerable she had become where Russ's work was concerned shocked her. Where had her objectivity gone? Was this the kind of feeling Russ confessed to having about the risks she took? She *knew* she never wanted to see Russ facing that tiger again. Though the whole situation had been an accident and Monarch had been reacting out of fright rather than intent to harm, she was glad the Bengal had made his last public appearance. She could handle the risks of everyday living and even the extraordinary risks sometimes involved in Russ's profession, but she couldn't deal with the death-defying chances of working an animal like Monarch.

Amazed at where her thoughts had taken her, Jade stared out the car window, realizing how wrong she had been about Russ's comments on her career. For the first time, she began to view her globe-trotting in a different light.

Before Jade could carry her self-examination any further, Con turned into the small space in front of their trailer. He parked, got out and came around to help.

"Damn," Russ swore when Con accidentally bumped him.

Jade slipped the cane the nurse had given her into Russ's hand. "This is probably better," she suggested, watching him carefully while gesturing Con to back away until Russ got his balance.

The camper door opened as Russ took his first step toward it. Sandra stood on the threshold, anxiously monitoring their progress.

"I've cleaned up. I hope you don't mind," she explained when Russ finally made it inside. "I made some soup, too."

"You're a lifesaver," Jade replied gratefully. Having had few friends, it was all the more special to find how important they could be in a crisis.

Con tucked an arm around Sandra's waist. "Let's go, honey." He glanced at Jade. "Call us if you need us."

She nodded, more interested in watching Russ make his way down the narrow hall to bed. She barely heard the door shut behind the couple. Following Russ, she pulled the covers down so he could stretch out. She eased into a sitting position beside him.

"The doctor said the shot would make you sleepy. Would you rather eat or get cleaned up before you zonk out?"

Russ gazed at her, forcing his eyes to focus properly. He was so sleepy he could barely understand her words. Whether it was a trick of the light or the painkiller, he saw something in her eyes he had hoped for and never expected to see. Love. For him. It was an illusion, but right now he was in the mood to believe in illusions.

"What I'd really like is for you to hold me again," he said huskily.

Jade shook her head, loving him more than she thought possible. "After, I promise." She had to be practical, for both of them.

It took too much energy to argue. "Soup first, I guess."

Driven by her love, Jade leaned forward to brush a kiss over his lips.

"What's that for?" he asked when she raised her head, her hazel eyes glowing.

"Because you didn't grouch at me like I suspect you did at the hospital staff," she teased gently, because she didn't dare be serious.

"I don't grouch," he denied indifferently, not really paying attention to her words. Instead, he was experiencing the new gentleness in her. He had seen Jade in many guises but never this one.

"That's not the impression I got," she disagreed, getting to her feet.

He caught her hand before she could leave him. "I should have said this sooner. Thank you for what you did this afternoon. You're some kind of woman, Jade Hendricks. You took on a tiger for me, and I'll never forget it." He lifted her hand to his lips and placed a kiss in the center of her palm. "I learned something these past few hours. I was wrong. About you and your work."

Jade could have cried from the irony. Just when she had realized she did feel excitement at danger, drinking from it as one did from a canteen of springwater, Russ changed his mind.

"You were right all along. I do take unnecessary risks. And I did love it. Too much, perhaps." She could give him this even if she could not stay with him. She pulled her hand free. "You made me see that, and I'll never forget that as long as I live." She made herself smile. "So we're even."

Twelve

You're what?"

Daryl's voice roared out of the phone. Jade winced, holding the receiver away from her ear. "Calm down, Daryl. You heard me. I'm not getting on that plane, revolution or no. Not until I help Russ get that tiger back to his ranch. I explained the accident to you and what the doctor said."

Daryl wasn't appeased. "Call that Sam person. He can fly up. Hell, if you weren't there that's what he and Blackwell would do. Do you realize what you're passing up? This uprising is so hot that even Washington is steaming about it. And you've been requested to go in. The only damn American and a woman, at that. Think of the prestige, what it will mean to your credibility factor."

Jade tried to be patient. This was the first time she had ever refused such a plum assignment, or any assignment. Daryl was only doing his job. "I won't change my mind," she said firmly, becoming more determined by the moment. "I'll fly out of Palm Beach tomorrow if I have to, but I'm not going to leave Russ in the lurch."

"What's going on down there besides that article? I never thought doing me a favor would turn into such a problem. All I asked you to do was to go to Florida and do a piece for one magazine. Was that so tough? Was that too much to ask in all the years I've been your mailing address, your contact with the picture-buying world and the man in the life of your best friend? Did I ask you to change anything about your personality? Did I expect anything of you but doing your job? And what do I get? You don't even sound like yourself." He came up for air then spoke again. "You aren't falling for that guy, are you?" he demanded suspiciously.

Jade had been silent through the tirade. She knew from experience it was a waste of effort to interrupt Daryl when he got in a temper. But the last part of his remarks caught her on the raw. "No, I'm not falling for him," she retorted swiftly if not truthfully. "You know I never leave a job half done. I'm not finished here, that's all." Had she put enough conviction in her reply to convince the agent? The sound of Irene's voice in the background brought a frown to Jade's face. That's all she needed. Once Irene got into the act she wouldn't have a chance. "Listen, friend, I have to go."

"Oh, no you don't," Irene said, having wrested the phone from Daryl. "Daryl's hopping around here like a demented chicken. Is he right? Did you and Russ hit it off? I knew it. I just knew it. I told you Russ was as sexy as sin. What does he think about you? Is this why you're turning down the job? Thank God. It sounds like a killer. I wouldn't touch it with a barge pole. Shut up, darling. I'm trying to talk."

The spate of questions and answers continued without any input from Jade. Irene had a habit of talking even when she should have been listening. Jade knew that she would have to wait for Irene to wind down before attempting to say anything.

"So how long are you staying? Has he proposed yet? Do I get to be maid of honor? I do not have to be married to be in the wedding, Daryl. Who knows, she and Russ might just beat us to the altar. Neither one of them are slow when it comes to something they want so stop raining on my parade."

The last bit got to Jade. Patience was one thing. Letting Irene think a wedding was on the horizon was an entirely different matter.

"There won't be a wedding. I told Daryl everything. I'm only staying long enough to help Russ get the tiger back to his ranch. I'll be flying out of Florida for Central America just as soon as I can get a plane."

"You're a fool, my girl. I set you up with the sexiest man, outside of Daryl, I know, and this is what you do with a golden opportunity. If you were standing right here beside me I would shake you until your teeth rattled."

Irritated at Irene's continued obtuseness, Jade snapped, "You did not set me up. I'm down here working. On assignment, remember?"

"And who do you think convinced Daryl to talk you into this job?"

"Aren't you forgetting that little matchmaking exercise you started pulling the minute I landed in New York? I know you and Daryl are happy about getting married. I'd be surprised if half the population of New York doesn't know the way you two carry on, but that doesn't mean I wanted to take the plunge myself. If it hadn't been for all those hints and the matchmaking I would've taken my vacation." The moment the words were out, Jade got a sinking feeling in the pit of her stomach.

"Exactly."

The satisfaction in Irene's voice was clear. "That wasn't funny, Irene," Jade murmured, too angry to even lash out. She had known Irene liked behind-the-scenes plotting and planning the way most children loved ice cream, but Jade had never known her to turn her efforts in her direction.

Irene heard the pain in Jade's voice and frowned, suddenly worried. She had meant to help not hurt. "Are you all right? I thought I was doing the right thing. You need someone, Jade. You just don't see it." The defense popped out as she began to realize what she might have done. "I didn't mean to hurt you. I love you like a sister."

"Whatever you meant, your lovely little plan succeeded. But what you forgot, my friend, is that Russ and I aren't the same kind of people. In all your planning, didn't it occur to you that neither of us could live the way the other does?"

"You could compromise," Irene rushed to supply.

"How? Which one of us gives up his work or changes it completely?" She sighed, leaning her head against the dirty glass of the phone booth. "I love you, Irene. You're the closest thing I've got to a family except for my father. But right now I don't like you at all."

With that she hung up the phone. She stayed slumped against the wall, letting the realization of how she and Russ had been maneuvered sink into her mind. She wasn't the only one paying a price for Irene's meddling. Russ was, too. And it was all her fault. Pushing herself erect, she faced what couldn't be changed. Tomorrow would see Russ free of her. That at least she could give him.

Jade stared out the trailer's small side window, watching the dawn push through the darkness. Russ lay still in her arms, his breath fanning her throat. She had been awake most of the night. And except for the time she had made the phone call to Daryl while Conner stayed with Russ she had been right here, holding Russ's restless body so he could sleep. He had gotten rest but she had had none. Thoughts chased futilely through her head. Images blending with reality. Love overlaying loneliness. Questions with no answers.

"I can feel you thinking," Russ whispered, his voice rough with sleep.

Startled, Jade glanced away from the window as he lifted his head. "You should rest a little longer. It's too early to be up," she murmured, ignoring his comment. She brushed back the hair ruffled across his brow, her fingers lingering for a moment in the silky strands.

"Probably," he agreed, before rolling carefully onto his back and drawing her against him. "But I wanted to watch the sunrise and you. Do you mind?" Cradling her face against his shoulder, he focused on the grayness framed in the window.

"No." She couldn't have refused him now. Not knowing that soon she wouldn't be able to hold him ever again. Jade inhaled his scent as she watched the day begin. The last one of their time together. She ached to tell him of her love but knew she would not. Better to let him think it was passion and desire she felt.

"I love you." The words were quiet, the emotion calmed by the feel of her in his arms. For a moment he had her. For a moment she was his, the restlessness that drove her soothed away.

"I was afraid you did." When his brows rose at her wording, she explained. "It was the only thing that made any sense. No matter how many times I said no to you, you always made me change my mind." She lifted her head to stare into his eyes. "I want to love you." She couldn't give him the words, but she could give him pleasure, her touch and, if he but knew it, her love.

Russ held her eyes and read the depth of her need to give of herself. Somehow, he knew she was offering him more than the passion of her body. "Gladly," he gasped, freeing her to touch him any way she chose. Lying back, he watched the desire and love showing clearly in her eyes glow brighter. She had not spoken the words but he found it didn't matter.

When she bent to touch her lips to his, he drank her taste as though this was his first and last sip. When she

stroked him with the gentleness of a summer breeze,
he made no effort to control the pleasured quickening
of his response. Delicacy gave way slowly to passion
until the storm of wanting caught them in its vortex.
The sky flared pink with the flames of the day's beginning as one they reached the searing pinnacle of
fulfillment.

Russ held her as she lay quivering in the after-
shock, her body a fluid, pliant warmth heating his
skin. There were no words left to him. Seconds ticked
by in silence until finally Jade eased out of his arms.
She would tell him now. She couldn't leave it a moment longer.

"I won't be going back to the ranch with you. I have
enough for the article." She looked out the window,
unable to look at him. "I'll help you get Monarch
home and then I'm leaving. Daryl has an assignment
for me."

Russ froze, staring at her back. There was more
than what she was telling him. Did she think a few
impersonal words would make him accept their parting? "What kind of assignment?"

"Does it matter?" She looked at him then. "I'm
going. I *want* to go."

"Damn you, Jade!" he said harshly. "You would
throw us away!" She didn't move or flinch from his
anger. She only watched him, taking what he dished
out as though she deserved his condemnation. That
angered him more, and his hands clenched into fists,
but he didn't move. If he had he would have pulled her
down on the bed and taken them both through the
fires of hell itself to prove to her she had to acknowledge the words she would not say. He knew she loved

him as surely as he knew her body. But she held those three words back, stealing his right to share even that much of her life.

He closed his eyes against the truth he read in hers. By the time he opened them again, she had collected her clothes and retreated to the bathroom.

Jade didn't think and refused to feel. She silently moved through the trailer, getting breakfast and cleaning up. She had said and done everything she could and some things she shouldn't. She existed in a limbo that allowed for functioning without demanding reality.

Because of Russ's leg and the need for as much immobility as possible, Jade was left with doing the greater share of the tasks involved in getting Monarch on the truck that would take them all to the airport. Once there, the charter people took over and in amazingly short time they were airborne. She knew Russ's leg was somewhat painful, although he denied the need for any medication. The hours of the flight passed with little conversation. Everything that could be said had been.

When the plane touched down at Palm Beach International, Jade felt reality come crashing down on her. This was it. Another few minutes and she would never see Russ again. She glanced across at Russ, but he wasn't looking at her. His eyes were on the tiger pacing the cage as though he hated the bars.

The cargo door opened letting in the Florida sun, heat and humidity. Jets, taking off and landing, filled the afternoon with eerie screams. Jade heard it all and noticed none of it. She followed Russ and Monarch down the ramp as they reversed the loading procedure. Sam was waiting by the truck, a worried look on his face. He brightened considerably when he saw Russ moving under his own power.

Jade hefted her duffel bag over her shoulder, waiting only until Russ latched Monarch into his cage on the back of the truck. "I'm going now," she said, staring up at him.

Russ met her eyes, inclining his head. "Have a good flight."

Sam jumped to the ground. "What do you mean, going? Where?"

"She has an assignment," Russ replied for her, his bitterness slipping through for an instant.

"Where? Doing what?" Sam demanded in surprise. "How long you gonna be gone? When are you coming back?"

"I'm not coming back." Jade made herself say the words.

"Why not?"

Russ leaned against the cage and folded his arms across his chest. His thigh was throbbing from the strain of standing, but he wouldn't have moved if his life depended on it. "Don't look at me. I don't know why she won't stay."

"I can't stay," Jade snapped, irritated with both of them. "And besides, you haven't asked me to."

"Have, too."

"Where else would you go, girl?" Sam asked, glancing from one to the other. Something was seriously wrong. "You fit in at Hideaway, and you know it's a sight better than hurrying around the world sticking that camera of yours in other people's business. You go to places that would turn my hair white.

Like that place in Central America that the papers are so full of right now. A person could get killed in situations like that." He stopped, clearly seeing that he had said something that Jade would rather he hadn't. Before he could voice his suspicions, Russ did.

"Is that where you're going?" Russ looked at her, his eyes narrowed in concentration. He knew it was true before she inclined her head. He moved then, coming down the ramp with a speed that denied his injury. He took her shoulders and turned her to face him. "I read about the damn coup in the paper on the flight down. It's a bloodbath. Are you out of your mind?"

"They asked for me."

"I don't care." He bit the words out, so angry he didn't care he might be infringing on her freedom. All he could think about was her getting hurt, perhaps killed, and he wouldn't even know unless he read it in the papers.

"Tell them you changed your mind. Take another assignment if you must, but forget this one."

"I can't. If I do I'll know why. And where will I stop? Will every job suddenly look too dangerous? You work with Monarch. Tell me now you'll never step in his cage again, never expose yourself to injury." She waved at his bandaged leg. "Do that and I'll back down."

He grimaced, hating her words because they held too much truth. "You know I'll work with him again, even though he's retired."

She shook off his hold and bent to pick up the duffel bag. "And I'll get on that plane. I'll cover this story because I can't do any less. It's the way I'm made."

She turned and started to walk away.

"Catch her," Sam ordered, unable to understand why Russ wasn't going after her.

"No." Russ watched her go. "She's right. And if you think about it you'll know it." She was so beautiful. Slender, tall, graceful. She had too much courage for her own good. Admiration and love filled him despite the worry in his eyes. "If you get yourself hurt I'll haunt you for the rest of your life," he called after her. He couldn't let her leave with anger between them.

Jade turned, smiling through her tears. "I love you." She whispered the words and saw him hear them and take a step toward her then stop. She turned and sprinted for the terminal. She had given her last gift to the man who had given her so much.

"You should have stopped her. You love her. I wouldn't have let Emma go like that. What is it with you two? Anyone with eyes in his head could tell what you both want."

"Can it, Sam," Russ said wearily without turning from his study of the passing scenery. "You've been on my neck for the past thirty-five miles. Give it a rest. I did everything I could but tie her down."

"You should have done that, too, if that's what it took. Crazy female's going to get herself killed."

Russ's head snapped up. Where Sam's continual nagging hadn't prodded his temper, Sam's stating of his fear did. "Will you shut up? Don't you think I know that? I hate where she's going, but I can't cage her. She either comes to me freely or she doesn't come at all."

Sam cast him a quick look. He grimaced, angry at himself. "I'm sorry, son. I didn't think."

Russ waved the apology away. "Forget it. Just drive. The sooner we get home the better."

"Why don't you turn on the radio? It'll give me something to occupy my mind so I don't think of stupid things to say for the next five miles."

Russ did as he suggested, more out of consideration for Sam than because he wanted the music. He had never felt so empty, so alone in his life. Even when they turned onto the road that would end at the house, he felt no sense of homecoming, no pride in what he had created. What did it matter what he accomplished if there was no one to share his triumph?

Jade was gone. He was here. No future and a past that hurt too much to remember.

Sam pulled to a stop in front of the barn, saying nothing. They got out together and set about moving Monarch from his cage to the compound.

"Emma will have supper ready at the regular time if you want to rest for a bit," the older man suggested quietly.

Leaning on his cane, Russ gazed at the two reunited tigers. "I'll be in in a while," he replied without turning around. He heard Sam walk away, leaving him to his thoughts.

His eyes were on the cats, but it was Jade he saw in his mind. Her smile when she had seen Monarch chasing the huge striped ball across the compound as if it were a ball of yarn. Her intense expression as she framed each camera shot and angle. The way she held her head as she gauged the sun and shadow. Her gliding walk. The way she could stay in the most awk-

ward positions trying to get that perfect shot and then
groan as though her back were breaking when she finally finished.

He turned away, needing some relief from his
memories. Each brought more pain, pain he couldn't
ease. Limping, he headed for the house. Maybe he
would find respite in sleep. Maybe his dreams were
safe, untouched by her presence. He never found out.
He got as far as lying down in the bed they shared. A
cold shower was no help nor was the almost desper-
ately normal meal he, Sam and Emma shared. Finally
the day was over, the house quiet and he was truly
alone. He roamed the rooms, pacing as Jade had
paced, finding no peace.

A stiff drink in one hand, his cane in the other, he
prowled the porch, peering into the night. No moon
illuminated the sky. No flash of light to dispel the
darkness. No woman to hold. No soft words to heal
the pain in his heart. No gentle touch to soothe his
throbbing leg. No Jade.

Thirteen

—

Jade stared down the lonely stretch of road, hating the slow-moving needle on the speedometer. Two more miles. Would it ever end? Maybe she was a fool, just as Daryl had called her when she'd phoned him from the airport to tell him she'd changed her mind. She had just given up a fantastic chance for an unknown future. Daryl didn't think she could do it, and maybe he was right. Maybe she couldn't settle down.

Then she remembered Irene's words. Her friend had snatched the phone from Daryl's hand. "Don't listen to this big lug, honey. Love makes bridges across the widest chasms. If you want Russ, go to him. Between you, you'll find a way. We did."

The tears had poured down Jade's face, and she hadn't cared. The angry words they'd had and the scheming Irene had done now meant nothing.

The car hit a bump, slamming down on the road hard enough to rattle every bolt. Jade hardly noticed. Decelerating, she turned onto the last stretch of road then hit the gas pedal. The car fishtailed. She brought it under control. Leaning forward, she stared into the darkness, straining for the first sight of his house.

Nothing. Blackness. Complete. Empty. Loneliness.

Soon, she hoped, no, she prayed, to be filled. Had she hurt him too much? Would Russ really want her? Could she stay? She had to remember he had said he loved her. He had offered no promises. She, who hated commitments, ties and vows found herself wishing Russ had tried to tie her to him. She would have had a lifeline, something to cling to now as she strode into a future that scared her, confused her and bewildered her. But more than that, it held her in a grip that wouldn't let go. She had to go to Russ. He was her love.

The headlights caught the first buildings. Tears stung her eyes. It would be the tigers' compound. She slammed on the brakes, sliding to a halt. A shadow moved on the porch. His name was on her lips as she tumbled out of the car. She took two running steps then stopped short, breathing deeply.

"Russ?"

He stood there, knowing she was real and not a figment of his imagination. He wanted to go to her and knew he couldn't. She had to make these last steps on her own. Their whole life together was at stake. "You drive like a maniac." She looked so vulnerable standing there. So fragile.

"I know." She closed the distance by a half step. Now that she was here she was without words. "I didn't go."

"Why?" They had had so many chances. This had to be the last one.

She shrugged, wishing he would take her in his arms. Maybe then she could be brave. "I don't know." She heard his indrawn breath and struggled to explain. "I couldn't leave you." Another step. "I actually got on the plane. I was in my seat and I looked out and knew I couldn't do it. Not then."

Russ let out his breath. She was scared, hurting, needing him. For the first time she was allowing her feelings to show, making herself vulnerable to him. He limped nearer. "And now? Regrets?"

"Yes. No. I don't know." Two paces this time. She lifted her hand. "Help me. Make me stay. I need you."

He shook his head. He would not take her this way. "I can't make you and, even if I could, I wouldn't. Your life. Your choice." He inhaled deeply, knowing he was hurting now more than ever before. "Stay because you want to, because you love me, because you can be happy here. No other way will do for us."

Jade stared at him, knowing he was right and wishing he weren't. "I'm afraid. I've never put down roots."

"And I've never faced the idea of letting the woman I love roam the world free." He held out his hand. Their fingers almost touched. "I'll give you your job because you need your liberty. Give me your love. Marry me. Have my children. Build a life with me."

Another step and her hand was in his. "You'll let me go?" She stared at him in wonder. She had not expected this. His generosity and understanding were more than she had known existed.

He pulled her to him. "All I ask is that you take care of yourself when I can't be with you. I closed Monarch's cage for good. He is retired." She had really come home to stay. She had made her choice out of love, and because he loved her he would see that she never regretted coming to him. He understood her commitment and the greatness in her. He would nurture both and protect her with all that he had in him. Jade was his love and his life.

His head bent, her lips lifted, a faint, trembling smile touching them as he kissed her. The moon came out of hiding to trace the silver streaks of tears upon her cheeks.

"I love you."

"Welcome home, gypsy."

"They want to do what?" Jade demanded blankly, her eyes fixed on her husband's smug face. She knew that expression, had seen it more than once in the past two years. Her fingers barely retained a grip on the phone she held as she tried to absorb Daryl's news.

"A documentary. You know, one of those programs to educate the masses," Daryl drawled. The sarcastic effect he intended was completely spoiled by the eager exuberance invading his every word.

Stunned, Jade plopped limply into Russ's lap, the receiver still clutched to her ear. "They want to do a documentary on *Forgotten Freedom*," she whispered to him. Leaning against his chest, she rested on his strength since her own had deserted her.

Russ smiled indulgently into the bemused eyes of his wife. It still amazed him that while she knew she was good she had yet to grasp just how good. Then he plucked the phone from her nerveless fingers as he slipped an arm around her waist and drew her tighter against him. "Yeah, she's all right," he assured the agent and now his friend. "She's just in a state of shock. I know it's good and you know it's good, but remember, Jade's never satisfied." He listened for a second longer then nodded. "I'll remind her to call you as soon as she surfaces," he promised before hanging up.

"I can't believe it," Jade breathed, tucking her head under his chin. The steady beat of his heart was in sharp contrast to her own.

"Honey, all of us told you how fantastic that book was. Your editor hardly changed a word. The publisher damn near broke every speed record in existence to get *Freedom* out on the stands." Unable to resist the temptation, he dropped a kiss on her parted lips before continuing. "One of these days you must accept that your creation is a bestseller in nonfiction."

Jade touched his cheek tenderly. How he had supported and encouraged her through the birth of *Forgotten Freedom*. It had been his idea to chronicle the heritage of the Royal Bengal tiger. How it had been slaughtered for its pelts, the attempted protection by governments that fought constant wars with poachers and the efforts of caring people to increase the population through breeding. A section on the history of

Monarch and Kismet had been widely acclaimed as it brought to light the work circus people did to care for and breed these special animals.

Russ had been with her every step of the way. He had helped her research the material when his schedule permitted. He had even journeyed with her to Nepal to visit the largest Bengal tiger reserve in the world. In a way, their trip had been a second honeymoon—no, an ongoing extension of their first, she corrected herself silently. Their days had been spent working, but their nights had been a celebration of love and life in each other's arms.

"No regrets, love?" Russ asked huskily.

She shook her head. "No, how could I have? I have you, a beautiful circle of friends, a home and a commitment worth fighting for. I still travel, but we're either together or you're here waiting for me when I get back. I have the best of all possible worlds." She really meant all she said. The wind was finally stilled, touching the land, sinking into its life-giving surface. Ties and promises no longer frightened her. She had given a commitment to Russ and in the giving learned the true meaning of freedom. Like the tigers she had grown to love, she had learned the cage was more than a home with bars. It was warmth, protection from nature's elements, approval and insurance for the future.

"What about you? I'm not like other wives. I never will be."

"You're what I wanted and all that I wanted. I love you." Russ caught her close, remembering for one fleeting second the agony of thinking her gone forever. It still gave him nightmares to realize how close they had come to losing each other.

"Don't think about it, darling," Jade whispered, slipping her arms around him. She knew and understood the fear that haunted him. It was a mirror image of her own. They were strong people but with the other they were also vulnerable and as defenseless as children. And they had almost let the future slip away from them.

"Maybe I'll forget when we celebrate our ninetieth anniversary," he offered, gazing at her with every emotion unmasked for her to see.

She smiled, her eyes cloudy with a woman's mystery. "You'll forget before that, I can promise you." She nipped his chin playfully. "In fact, I suspect you'll be wishing you had let me go in about seven months," she pronounced with a laugh.

"When the North Pole melts," he muttered, barely hearing her words through the desire flickering to life in his body. He captured her lips, drinking deeply of the wine-rich taste of his mate. His hand found her bare breast beneath her shirt, cupping the fullness possessively. She whimpered, a cry so similar to the tiny sounds of Kismet's tiger cubs, he lifted his head to smile at her. In that second, her words finally penetrated, stealing the amusement from his lips and leaving behind astonishment.

"You're pregnant," he announced as though making a great discovery.

"I know," Jade agreed complacently before wriggling enticingly in his lap. "And I'm going to get a lot pregnanter so we'd better make love while we can."

"There's no such word as pregnanter," he murmured dazedly, frowning at her calm attitude. She was going to have a baby. Wasn't she supposed to be sick or something? He stared down at her flat belly, suddenly realizing how tightly he was holding her. Instantly he released her, praying he hadn't squashed something important.

"What's wrong, darling? You look absolutely green," Jade demanded, feeling the change and not understanding it.

"Shouldn't you be in bed or something?" he asked, ignoring her question.

Jade stared at him in puzzlement. "That's just what I had in mind, and I thought you did, too." He was acting most peculiarly.

"We can't," he muttered, sliding gingerly to his feet with her in his arms. "Mothers-to-be need pampering."

Jade looped her hands behind his neck, hiding a smile as the light dawned. Her big, strong male was coming unglued over the prospect of her being with child. Heaven alone knew how many deliveries he had witnessed, had even assisted in. Looking at his face, no one would believe he was either calm or experienced. It was going to be an interesting seven months, she decided in silent amusement, cuddling closer.

"So pamper me," she commanded as they entered their bedroom. Holding on when he would have deposited her gently on the bed, she stared him straight in the eye. "I want to make love right now."

Russ froze, his eyes growing gold with desire. "I might hurt you. I'm not always gentle," he pointed out huskily. To hold her, to fuse his body with her knowing that between them his child rested, was an experience he ached to have. His wife, soon to be the mother of his baby. Jade. His Jade.

"You've never once hurt me," she reminded him, tugging on his shoulders demandingly. "You're everything I need now and always. And soon there'll be three of us." She wouldn't allow even his scruples to come between them.

Russ came down beside her, pulling her on top of him so he could see her face. "Three of us or ten. No one will ever take your place. My love, my own gypsy wind." His vow rang with the depth of his love. The man who tamed the wind and held it in his hand, close to his heart.

*   *   *   *   *

Silhouette Intimate Moments

MORE THAN A MIRACLE
by Kathleen Eagle

This month, let award-winning author Kathleen Eagle sweep you away with a story that proves the truth of the old adage, "Love conquers all."

Elizabeth Donnelly loved her son so deeply that she was willing to sneak back to De Colores, an island paradise to the eye, but a horror to the soul. There, with the help of Sloan McQuade, she would find the child who had been stolen from her and carry him to safety. She would also find something else, something she never would have expected, because the man who could work miracles had one more up his sleeve: love.

Enjoy Elizabeth and Sloan's story this month in *More Than A Miracle*, Intimate Moments #242. And if you like this book, you might also enjoy *Candles in the Night* (Special Edition #437), the first of Kathleen Eagle's De Colores books.

ATTRACTIVE, SPACE SAVING BOOK RACK

Display your most prized novels on this handsome and sturdy book rack. The hand-rubbed walnut finish will blend into your library decor with quiet elegance, providing a practical organizer for your favorite hard-or soft-covered books.

Only $9.95

Approximately 16" x 8" when assembled

Assembles in seconds!

To order, rush your name, address and zip code, along with a check or money order for $10.70* ($9.95 plus 75¢ postage and handling) payable to *Silhouette Books*.

Silhouette Books
Book Rack Offer
901 Fuhrmann Blvd.
P.O. Box 1396
Buffalo, NY 14269-1396

Offer not available in Canada.

BKR-2A

*New York and Iowa residents add appropriate sales tax.

Silhouette Desire

COMING NEXT MONTH

TALES OF THE RISING MOON
A Desire trilogy by Joyce Thies

MOON OF THE RAVEN—June
Conlan Fox was part American Indian and as tough as the Montana land he rode, but it took fragile yet strong-willed Kerry Armstrong to make his dreams come true.

REACH FOR THE MOON—August
It would take a heart of stone for Steven Armstrong to evict the woman and children living on his land. But when Steven met Samantha, eviction was the last thing on his mind!

GYPSY MOON—October
Robert Armstrong met Serena when he returned to his ancestral estate in Connecticut. Their fiery temperaments clashed from the start, but despite himself, Rob was falling under the Gypsy's spell.

Don't miss any of Joyce Thies's enchanting
TALES OF THE RISING MOON,
coming to you from Silhouette Desire.